Mysterious circles appear in the cornfields down Shafton way, sparking a feud with a neighbouring hamlet, creating a nice little earner for a favoured few, causing a major career adjustment for a senior Government official, and damn near wrecking the Japanese economy.

What on Earth would visitors from another planet make of it all? . . .

SHAFTON CIRCLES

Ray Bullock

Calleva Publishing

Published in Great Britain by

Calleva Publishing The Butts Silchester Hampshire RG7 2QD

ISBN 0 952 1051 1 X

Set in Palatino 10/11 by Ann Buchan (Typesetters), Shepperton

Cover Illustration: Paul Sample
Cover Design: A & A Design

Printed and bound in Great Britain by
Cox & Wyman Ltd., Reading

chapter 1

That blue planet over to our right looks interesting, thought Yttrium, peering through sleep-encrusted eyes, it seems to have all the essential elements.

You could well be right, agreed Argona, if the blue really is water then we can be sure of hydrogen and oxygen, and the big star is close enough to provide bags of energy. She rinsed her huge, deep purple eyes with refreshingly cold water, and set her mind towards the blue planet.

Here, hold on, thought Yttrium, I was merely speculating. I could well be wrong you know, it wouldn't be the first time. Hadn't we better think this through, I mean, you never know what we might find down there. You really must learn to curb your impulsive instinct, my dear, it could land us both in all kinds of danger.

For the love of Strontium, reflected Argona, stifling a yawn, must you always put a damper on everything? This is the likeliest spot we've found in ages and all you can do is dither. Now come on, pull yourself together man, we're going in.

Had he been endowed with a voice, Yttrium would have undoubtedly been moved to a screaming fit at this juncture. As it was, his telepathic channel to Argona was jammed with foreboding — right up to panic pitch

— because the recipient of his anxiety wasn't taking a blind bit of notice.

She needed all her concentration to guide their vehicle on its newly-selected course, a destination which, according to her calculations, would at least be a good spot to celebrate her 350th birthday. It might even prove sufficiently hospitable to tarry a little longer, to relax a little and let one's hair down for a while. Life's too short, she mused, to be constantly travelling.

Not that life on their native planet, Strontium, was anything but interminably long, and terminally boring. That's why they'd taken to the skies in the first place, that and the weather.

Strontium's figure of eight orbit around its twin stars of Castor and Pollux was an elongated ellipse, bringing it very close to each of them in turn before being hurtled out into the blackness once more. Just at the point when the gravitational pull was at its weakest the weather would be quite nice for a few days. Very dark, but at least the sea was calm and land quakes subsided for a while, but then the whole damned process started off yet again.

It was like being at the very top of a gargantuan roller coaster, just hanging there, knowing full well what was coming next. Slowly Strontium would pick up speed, the days becoming shorter as she began to spin more quickly, the eerie purple glow of Castor looming larger and larger, filling the sky as they approached the perihelion.

By this time Strontium was spinning so fast the cycle of night and day became little more than a stroboscopic blur, while Castor's immense energy turned the seas into steam and great fissures appeared in the groaning, creaking land. A short period of calm would follow as, almost equally balanced between the gravitational pull of Castor and Pollux, the spin rate would relax a little, giving people time to clear up and get their dwellings in order for the big winter.

As they passed the freezing cold Pollux, spinning once more like a whirling dervish, the star's icy geen light refracted through the frozen steam into a thousand hues, the wavelengths of which were only truly discernible through huge purple eyes. The combined effect of mind-blowing colours and stroboscopic daylight cycles put all the inhabitants of Strontium into a deep trance, in which they would remain for the long journey out into the darkness and back again, waking in time to watch Castor melt the ice, and for the whole cycle to begin again.

After more than three hundred years of this, however, Yttrium and Argona were more than a little pissed off. Millions of like-minded Strontians had cleared off over the millenia and, from images received through the telepathic network, they were having the time of their lives. Even so, Yttrium took some persuading.

It's all very well leading the free and easy space lifestyle, he thought, but what if it all goes wrong? Once they got more than a few weeks away from Strontium breakdown services would become almost non-existent, and you couldn't just sit on the nearest comet thumbing a lift, people travelling at those kind of speeds just wouldn't stop. Their vehicle had, after all, seen better days.

Only last year, on their holiday to the nearby planet of Tellurium, the damn thing had refused to take off. The only time it's safe to leave Strontium is at the furthest point in its orbit around Castor — when the seas are still and gravity is at its weakest — only then can the vehicle's density adjuster render it lighter than its surroundings, lifting it slowly away from mother Strontium.

On that occasion the plasma jelly from which the vehicle was constructed had become a glutinous mass — Argona had left it outdoors, yet again, in the heat of the Castor passover — and it had taken Yttrium ages, trying to soften it with a Radon torch, before it would float freely.

After yet another year on that endless roller coaster, however, even Yttrium had to admit there must be a better way to spend the next five or six centuries. Maybe they'd come back here to retire, to put their feet up for their final few flings around Castor and Pollux but, for the time being at least, they would enjoy the freedom of the open skies.

Argona couldn't wait to get away. All through the long winter, as Yttrium lay in his techni-coloured trance, she had practiced her mental exercises — over and over again. Telekinetic energy is the only propellant available or, indeed, necessary on Strontium these days, and to power a vehicle through thought processes alone requires skill, determination and immense concentration.

These were certainly not lacking in Argona, nor indeed in any true green-blooded Strontian, but they had to be kept honed to perfection. Just a solitary, momentary lapse of concentration and you could be sucked into one of the countless black holes which litter the universe, condensed into anti-matter and spewed out the other side. Nothing good ever came out of one of those things.

When the day finally dawned she was ready. The vehicle had been garaged during the hot spell, Yttrium had filled all the rotted patches with fibre jelly, and there was sufficient food concentrate and condensed water on board to keep an army alive for years. Or so they thought.

Promising to keep telepathic channels open for their friends and relatives, the pair scrambled aboard, sealed the jelly, and took to the sky. Happiness, thought Argona, is Strontium in your rear viewfinder. Yttrium wasn't so sure.

Ned Thrubwell, on his rusty old sit up and beg bike, with its three-speed Sturmey Archer gears — only one of which worked — was on an errand for his employer, Mrs Featherstonehaugh.

She had a letter to be delivered to Lord Hampton, in person, and didn't want to entrust such an important missive to the postal services. The personal courier service provided by her old retainer was far more reliable, despite the torrential rain, besides which it was cheaper.

The main road through to Hampton Magna was flooded at the Hatch End ford and, if he'd tried to get across he'd undoubtedly have been swept away by the raging river. And if he didn't want a twenty-odd mile detour through the hills, the only route available was through the hamlet of Farthing Fflitch. A twenty-odd mile detour, up and down those bloody hills with one gear, and in this weather, was the last thing Ned wanted — well almost.

Farthing Fflitch was not a safe place to be, not for a Shaftonite on his own. Grown men had been known to disappear down there, never to be seen again. Rumour has it they'd been eaten alive by the Fflitches, torn limb from limb by the men of this strange hamlet while the children fought over the discarded bits, stuffing their fat, blood-soaked little faces.

Be that as it may, if he went over the hills Ned would certainly not be back in Shafton until well after closing time and, as he enjoyed his regular drop of Haymaker at the Shafton Arms, Farthing Fflitch it would have to be. Checking to make sure he had money in his old jacket pocket, to pay the toll for crossing the rickety, ancient bridge, Ned hunched his shoulders against the driving rain and pedalled like fury.

The bridge had been in the Fflitch family for years, ever since the eighteenth century, when the toll for crossing was a farthing — hence the hamlet's name. That, together with a few fields, and the fishing rights on this world famous piece of trout river, represented the entire assets of the Fflitches — a very close family who didn't take kindly to strangers, that's for sure. If your name wasn't Fflitch, you weren't to be trusted.

Forty six souls resided in the hamlet of Farthing Fflitch, and every one of them was a Fflitch through and through, each with five fingers on the left hand, as well as a thumb — a characteristic which had ensured, over the centuries, that not a single farthing slipped out of their hands into the river, or anywhere else for that matter. What the Fflitches had, they kept — and they kept it within the family.

It's been many years since any alien DNA has infiltrated the Fflitch blood line, and it was the last donation that particular, luckless, wretch would ever make. It's said that the offending organs were pickled in ram's urine before being nailed to the turnpike, there to act as a reminder to all foreign swains and would-be suitors that you don't mess with the Fflitches.

Although the lane leading into the village could, if push came to shove, just about accomodate a car, the Fflitches had erected a sign — at their own expense mind you — declaring to all and sundry, that the road was unsuitable for motor vehicles.

And if that wasn't enough to deter the unwary traveller, a few hundred yards further on was a cattle grid, two of the central bars of which were missing. Frankie

Fflitch, the only member of the family who could rustle up enough brain power, on one of his more lucid days, to pass a driving test, carried the missing bars in his Land Rover. Over the years the Land Rover had more than earned its keep by towing unsuspecting drivers off that cattle grid.

As it was garaged in Farthing Fflitch and, because of the width of the lane could only tow them in the direction of the hamlet, visitors would inevitably end up there from time to time. The bridge itself was far too weak to take even the lightest car these days and so day trippers, who had perhaps set out to find a scenic route to Winchester for a day's shopping and sight seeing, found themselves incarcerated.

Now if you were stuck in that position, you would undoubtedly want to make the best of a bad job and take a look around. You might want to admire pretty thatched rooves atop whitewashed cottages, enjoy a cream tea in a quaint little tea room by the side of the river, or perhaps take a stroll along some leafy, sun-dappled lane to while away an hour or two in God's own little piece of Hampshire. There are plenty of pretty little spots in this fair County where you would find just that, and much more — but this isn't one of them.

Most of the properties are said to have been unfit for human habitation when the Fflitchs built them in the eighteenth century. They've deteriorated a bit since then. Some of the original oak roofing trusses are still to be seen, with bits of corrugated iron and plastic sheeting nailed to them, and one of the properties even had some whitewash thrown at it once. The impulsive moment had passed, however, before any serious good was done.

You'd undoubtedly find the odd, well-used, tea bag amongst the rubbish littering the river bank — waiting for a decent rainstorm to carry it into the river — but that's about as close as you'd get to that thirst-quenching, quintessentially English institution.

And as for leafy lanes, forget it. There are, of course, several public rights of way, but only the foolhardy would try to exercise their rights. Besides which the all-pervading, heady aroma of manure — only a little of which comes from the animals — is unlikely to enchant your senses.

The most sensible course of action would be to put your financial loss — the fortune Frankie charged for towing you off the cattle grid — down to experience and clear off as fast as you can. And don't worry about getting stuck on the cattle grid on your way out, Frankie will be waiting for you on the other side — the six digits of his left hand ready-cupped for your kind offering.

Ned had not been by this way for years. In his teens he'd once taken a shine to one of the spinsters Fflitch and had polished his boots, put on his Sunday Best clothes — positively wreaking of mothballs — and set off on his second-hand sit up and beg bicycle with three speed Sturmey Archer gears — two of which worked.

After removing his cap — which he wore back to front when cycling — and his bicycle clips, all of which he'd then stowed neatly away in his saddle bag along with his oilskins and sou'wester, he'd leaned the bike up against the front wall of his intended's hovel and gingerly knocked on the front door, smoothing down his brilliantined hair with the other hand at the same time.

Reply came there none so he'd knocked again, this time a little harder, but still without response. Undeterred he'd taken to banging with all his might on that door, a noise which would have woken the dead in Shafton let alone Farthing Fflitch, and that was his undoing. Upstairs the time-honoured, warm, greeting for strangers was almost ready for presentation.

How his mother had laid into him with the stropping belt when he'd returned home, still saturated in the contents of that chamber pot. It was a hiding and a half, one he'd never forget, and he'd not returned to the scene of his misfortune until this very day, more than half a century later.

And now, as he approached the hamlet, its familiar fragrance borne on the wind driving into his weather beaten, rain soaked face, he couldn't help wondering whatever happened to little Fenella Fflitch, the object of his lustful desires all those years ago.

The blue planet has a moon, thought Yttrium, maybe we should set down there for a while and take a good look at this place before jumping in feet first.

That won't be necessary, dear, thought Argona. Don't you remember the images we had from Iodina and Thulium a few years back? I'm sure it was this planet, it looks so familiar. They absolutely adored it, and they've been back several times since, so I think we should go for it. Besides, that big red planet isn't too far away, and I reckon those straight lines on it must be canals, can't logically be anything else, so at least we know there's water there. We can always head for that one if we're disappointed with the blue one.

Yttrium really couldn't decide whether they should make straight for the blue one, or hold station on its moon for a while. It seemed, however, that Argona had more than made up her mind and, what Argona wanted, Argona usually got — one way or another.

They'd been travelling for twelve years now, most of that time spent in hibernation snuggled together in the enveloping jelly which lined the interior of the vehicle, umbilically linked to the concentrated food and condensed water supply, and telepathically linked to the vehicle's control system.

Much of the mental input required for the occasional minor adjustments had been Argona's, Yttrium only being roused from the depths of his slumbers when danger or uncertainty lurked — when two heads are better than one — so it was understandable, perhaps, that she should be excited. And didn't she have a birthday coming up, he reflected, something he'd be more than a little unwise to forget.

Gradually winding down his telepathic output, so as not to arouse Argona's suspicions, he thought long and hard about what he could give her for a birthday treat. There was precious little on board the vehicle, so it would have to come from one of the planets. Maybe he could find something suitable on the blue one, some little memento of their visit. He cast his mind back to the images they'd received from Iodina and Thulium.

That's it, he realised, Iodina had been enthralled by a precious metal they'd discovered there, her images had been full of it, and Argona had been so impressed with the rare beauty of it. Not that there's any shortage of metals on Strontium and its neighbouring planets, but this one was something special, something the folks back home would positively rave about. He must try very hard to find her a nice piece of aluminium.

Right, it's decision time, thought Argona, the suddenness of her thought shaking Yttrium from his reverie, are we going straight in or do you really want to camp out on this lifeless looking moon?

Alright, you win, smiled Yttrium, but for goodness sake put us down gently — on the daylight side, if you please, so we can see just what we're getting ourselves into. There's plenty of water down there, some of those seas really are quite large, so perhaps a splashdown would be our best option, just in case we come in a little quickly. I don't mean to be critical, dear, but parking isn't one of your strong points now, is it?

Argona treated that little jibe with the contempt it deserved, besides it was better to try and ignore Yttrium when he was nervous, pandering to his anxiety only made him worse. She could feel the vehicle beginning to heat up a little now as they approached the outermost edge of earth's atmosphere.

Trimming back the jelly's edges to reduce unnecessary friction, and gradually elongating the vehicle's shape to that of a cigar, thereby easing their passage into the gaseous atmosphere now being encountered, she slowed right down to look for potential landing sites — landing being the operative word, she had absolutely no intention of splashing down anywhere, thank you very much.

There was certainly no shortage of land to choose from, but much of it looked far too dry for her liking. The seering heat from the big star would probably damage the jelly, maybe even bake it dry, so perhaps the equatorial land masses would be inadvisable. The polar regions looked far too cold, and would undoubtedly invoke Yttrium's innate hibernation instinct yet again, so she looked for somewhere cool, but not cold, and with sufficient water in the surface gases to stop the jelly from drying out.

Spotting an island which had great potential, she hovered over it to get a closer look. There was plenty of cloud cover, with an almost endless supply of further clouds in the South-Westerly winds, which blew gently in across the big sea. Those huge, purple, complex-lensed eyes, evolved over millions of years of having to deal with such variable conditions on Strontium, had no trouble seeing through the clouds, and the welcoming greenery of the land below was simply too much to resist.

Gently easing the vehicle down through the clouds, constantly adjusting its density relative to that of its new surroundings, and changing to a much flatter, disc shape to spread the weight as evenly and as smoothly as possible on the ground, Argona selected a flat, rectangular, golden coloured area on which to land.

Not bad, thought Yttrium grudgingly, feeling the jelly gradually compressing under his feet as their vehicle touched down for a perfect landing in the field of rain-soaked, sun-ripened corn. Argona smiled an exhausted, but none the less self-satisfied, smile at a job well done, and settled back for little well-earned, immensely deep, sleep.

Ned's jaw dropped open in sheer disbelief, his bottom lip left flapping in the strong, wet, South-Westerly wind.

chapter 2

"What the 'ell we gunna do now, babe, now me job's goin' down the swannee like?" fretted Joss, the worry of the last few weeks etched deeply into his fat little face, and the few remaining strands of ginger hair which graced his shining pate threatening to come out in sympathy.

"We've been in worse scrapes, babe," reassured his wife, "Something'll turn up, just you wait and see." The eternal optimism of Mr Micawber hardly became Fleur, who'd spent her entire married life doing the worrying for both of them, but right now she needed to at least appear unruffled — Joss needed her strength now more than ever.

When the Sticks first arrived in Shafton they had nothing, now they had a nice, comfortable home in The Olde Brewhouse, one of a pair of semi-detached cottages rented from the Shafton Manor Estate. That, at least, was something to be thankful for, and Fleur had a nice little side-line making clothes for friends and neighbours, that alone should help keep the wolf from the door for a while.

Joss' skills, like his brain cells, were few and somewhat far between, but he was one of life's triers. He'd tried labouring on building sites back home in Liverpool, but didn't like it. He'd tried emptying bins for the City Corporation, but got terrible lumbago. He'd tried playing guitar for a Mersey Sound rock band — The Bootles — but two gigs in three years were hardly going to set the music world alight.

He'd worked very hard at his present job at Prosser Prosthetics Plc, and had learned just about all there was to know about his particular plastic injection-moulding machine. There wasn't much you could teach Joss about knocking out plastic testicles, it had become almost second nature to him, but your average employer in the small Hampshire towns within commuting distance of Shafton had little use for such specialist skills.

His employer, Peter Prosser, had been caught red-handed importing cocaine in hollowed-out testes, made especially for the job by one J Stick Esq. It was only because the Judge, along with every single member of the jury, was more than ready to accept Counsel's submission of his client's ignorance — they could see, quite clearly, this was a quality he possessed in abundance — that had saved him facing the same long prison sentence now stretching out in front of the luckless Prosser.

But without Prosser at the helm the firm was sinking rapidly, and it was only a matter of time before the shutters would be going up, everybody knew that.

They talked of nothing else down at the Shafton Arms. Most of Shafton's residents either worked at Prossers, or had a friend or relative who did, so few were untouched by the problems besetting the company.

"Know anybody who wants to buy a pub?" enquired Georgie Smith, the landlord, through the side of his mouth. His enquiry was aimed solely at Ned, but it fell upon deaf ears — Ned's mind was elsewhere, about four miles hence in Farthing Fflitch.

"Oi, 'ee deaf ol' bugger, I be talkin' to 'ee" protested Georgie a little louder, but Ned's old eyes just continued staring into the bottom of his quart beer mug. They'd lost their familiar sparkle, thought Georgie, something must be deeply troubling his old friend.

"Ready for another, Ned — on the 'ouse like" he whispered quietly, just to see if there was anyone at home inside that worried old cranium.

"Ar go on then" responded Ned on auto pilot. The conscious part of his grey matter may be elsewhere, but that element responsible for essential functions, such as breathing, digestion, keeping the heart pumping and the beer coming, was not about to let him down.

"Come on me ol' mate" smiled Georgie, filling Ned's mug with Haymaker, "looks like 'ee seen a ghost or summat".

"Bain't no ghost, not what I seen" mumbled Ned, looking up at last, although avoiding Georgie's eyes like the plague, "this bugger was far from bloody dead".

"So was it after bein' da little people den?" quipped Paddy O'Toole. He never missed a thing, and if there was mockery to be made you could rest assured that Paddy would home in faster than an Exocet missile. "An' did dey beat ya to da pot of gold at da end of da rainbow again me ol' mate?" he laughed.

One by one the conversations around the bar ground to a halt. The assembled gathering new instinctively that something was wrong. It wasn't that Paddy was taking the piss out of old Ned, there was nothing new there, but that Ned wasn't responding — not even a "Sod off back to Ireland 'ee thick bugger", his automatic response when cornered. You could always rely on Ned to trot that one out at least once a night, but not tonight.

It was left to Georgie to break the ice with his "Leave

the poor bugger alone, 'tis probably 'is time of the month". The ensuing, polite, laughter acknowledging this crack fooled nobody. The bar room philosophers returned to putting the world to rights, but everyone knew there was something wrong with Ned. Very wrong indeed.

Come closing time Georgie shut the bar and called "Time, gentlemen, if you please" in his stern voice, the one he only used when he was expecting a visit from the local constabulary. There would be no 'afters' in the Shafton Arms tonight.

Needless to say, he wasn't expecting the Law to drop in unannounced tonight, otherwise he'd have known about it — years of pouring ale down PC Ronald Runstable's neck, much of it in the wee small hours of the morning, had ensured the only surprises he'd get would be for Christmas and his birthday. He did, however, want to get to the bottom of Ned's bit of bother.

"Now come on 'ee ol' bastard, bain't nobody 'ere but we, so out with it. Get it off 'ee chest mate" he urged, pouring another refill of Ned's mug. Slowly Ned summoned up courage, after all, if he couldn't tell Georgie, then who the sodding hell could he unburden himself on?

"Bain't never seen nothin' like it. Never 'ave, and never wants to again. Bigger than a bloody 'ouse it were —bigger than six soddin' 'ouses—but 'ouses don't just fall out the sky now do they?"

"Nar, course not mate. I can 'onestly say, with me 'and on me 'eart, I ain't never seen a 'ouse fall out the sky."

"But this bugger did. Well, not so much fall, more sort of, er, well, kind of, floated down — know what I mean?"

"Yeah, course I do me ol' mate, just sort of floated

down, real gentle like. Did it 'ave a parachute then, this 'ouse?"

"Weren't no bloody 'ouse, that's what I be tryin' to tell 'ee, but 'twas bigger than a 'ouse — bigger than a 'ole row of 'ouses. I tell 'ee mate, scared the shit out of I it did."

"I'll bet. An' what time would this 'ave been like?"

"Must 'ave bin 'bout arf past four. Why?"

"Well 'ee was alright when 'ee left 'ere lunchtime, never 'ad no more 'an eight pints, same as usual. Ain't been at they Shafton Roses again 'ave 'ee? Bain't no good for 'ee, specially when you'm of a certain age like."

"Nar, I ain't touched they since that copper told I it were bloody cannibals, what they kids smoke — whacky baccy like — an' even then I only ate it. Didn't arf make I fart though, summat terrible it did."

"An' it were daylight — when 'ee seen it then, this row of 'ouses like — so 'ee couldn't 'ave mistook it for summat else."

"I keeps tellin' 'ee, it weren't no row of bloody 'ouses, that's only 'ow big it were."

"Oh, right. Well what the 'ell did it look like then, this, this er, thing?"

"Well, it were green — bright green — an' all shiny. An' 'twas round, an' flat on the bottom. But bloody 'uge."

"So, it were big, green, round — but flat on the bottom — an' it floated down out the sky. An' did it 'ave little green men in it, with aerials on their 'eads? An' did it play weird tunes when it come in to land, 'ee knows, like that ther 'Close Counters' film?"

"Don't know what were in it — didn't bloody 'ang about to find out did I? They ain't taking I away for speriments, only to bring I back twenty years later with a green belly button — sod that for a game of soldiers. Bloody odd though, now 'ee come to mention it, there weren't no noise when it come into land, none at all — 'cept of course the wind, bloody windy it was, an' rainin'."

"So where did it land exactly, then, this big, round, flat at the bottom, green lump of metal?"

"That's summat else an' all. Bain't made of metal, more like some sort of jelly — all blubbery like. It come down in the cornfield, t'other end of Fairacre Farm, down by Farthin' Fflitch. I'll take 'ee to it now if 'ee like."

"Nar, not tonight me ol' mate, 'tis a bit late for I to be out lookin' for Martians. Tell 'ee what though, ol' Doctor Foster knows all 'bout they kind of things, now why don't 'ee drop by ther tomorrow mornin' an' 'ave a nice, long chat with 'e?"

Ned couldn't be absolutely certain — he never could be absolutely certain about anything after a night on the Haymaker — but he had a sneaking suspicion that, for some reason, Georgie didn't totally believe him. He couldn't put his finger on it, maybe it was just the smirk on his face — but then Georgie always had a smirk on his face, he was born like it — that made him suspect, deep down, his old friend needed to be convinced.

Georgie, on the other hand, hadn't had such a belly laugh for ages. He could hardly contain himself until Ned was well out of earshot, then the flood gates opened. Poor old Jill couldn't get a word out of him that night, nor anything else for that matter. He just lay in his bed, giggling, occasionally sitting up to catch his breath, and biting hard on the headboard as the tears rolled down his cheeks.

Now Georgie was never one for telling tales out of school. If you had a problem you could always confide in Georgie, in the certain knowledge that not only would he move heaven and earth to help you, but that nobody else would get to hear about it. This, however, was something else — something else completely.

Some people in this life have a penchant for holding their pudding out for custard and, in such circumstances, Georgie was very happy to oblige — with the biggest ladle you could possibly imagine. He'd never forgotten how Ned had ripped off half the village, that Christmas Eve, by betting them all they'd see a full moon on the Church roof on Christmas morning, then greeting their departure from midnight mass by dropping his trousers atop the roof — in the full glare of the spotlight.

That particular little score had yet to be settled, and tomorrow couldn't come quickly enough for Georgie.

With Argona sleeping like a baby, Yttrium was becoming curious about his new surroundings. Were the surface gases poisonous? Was the water drinkable? Was the planet inhabited and, if so, by what kind of beings? Would there be fresh food to be had? Twelve years of concentrated food coursing through one's veins — and nothing in one's belly — left one a mite peckish. How much concentrate did they have left anyway?

On checking the reservoir, deep in the interior jelly, he realised just how close they'd come to extinction. Just a few weeks more in hibernation and they'd have simply slipped into unconsciousness and died — as countless of their kind had before them — simply drifting about in the vastness for eternity or, at least, until they came within the gravitational pull of a black hole.

Surely it wasn't beyond the manufacturers of these vehicles to devise some kind of early warning system, something to bring the occupants out of hibernation when concentrate, or condensed water, was nearing the point of no return. He really must speak to someone about this when they returned home, it really wasn't good enough.

Trying to remain calm, so as not to transmit his mental state to Argona and awaken her, he decided to test the surface gases for noxious substances and sent out a plasma tentacle to collect a sample. Slowly the tentacle returned, passing a sizeable bubble of air, fresh from the Farthing Fflitch manure heap, into the interior for inspection.

It contained rather more nitrogen than the air on Strontium, but the oxygen level was adequate for their needs, and there was even a touch — but only a touch — of some of the gases found in abundance back home. Gases like Neon and Argon — Argona would be pleased.

Gradually releasing the bubble from the jelly, Yttrium placed his nose into the airflow and sniffed. Had his stomach been blessed with contents they would, by now, be lining the wall of the vehicle's interior. He had never smelled anything so disgusting in his entire life. Realising he had no option but to persevere, however, he released another whiff, then another, until he was able to eventually fill his lungs with the foul-smelling air.

He checked the background radiation of the planet, and found it to be reassuringly low, and the temperatures recorded during the period of daylight and at night were well within their comfort range. The planet had a very strong magnetic field, mainly running in a North-South direction, but there were some very interesting, if somewhat faint, energy lines criss-crossing all over the place. He resolved to investigate these further in due course but, for the time being and with his initial checks now completed, it was time to venture forth.

His checks had also revealed a great deal of activity across the spectrum of radio frequencies, indicating the existence of life forms — albeit of only level one or, at best, level two technological advancement — so he must keep his wits about him. Life forms of such low intellect were known to be still somewhat aggressive.

Gently parting the plasma jelly, he stepped out into the field of corn, the ears of which came right up to his round, wrinkled little chin, and immediately wretched as the obnoxious bouquet of the manure heap once again reviled his sensory organs. He wondered what kind of beings could live with such a malodorous stink, and concluded that noses would not be a part of their physical characteristics.

And then he saw it — his very first encounter with an Earth being. It was much smaller than Yttrium, no bigger than his hand in fact, and it seemed to be showing a very friendly interest in him. How odd, he thought, bending down to make a closer inspection, they appear to have noses after all — and quite sensitive ones at that. The little creature was sniffing around Yttrium's toes, seemingly quite enthralled by the concentrated essence of twelve bathless years.

Reaching down still further, and offering his empty, weaponless hands in a gesture of friendship, he was surprised to see the creature simply curl up into a very tight ball, its sharp little spines ready to inflict considerable discomfort to any being foolish enough to try and eat it.

Yttrium, of course, had no intention of eating the hedgehog. No matter how hungry he might be, the flesh of other living beings was simply not on a Strontian's menu, they'd given that up millions of years ago — hence their green colour. Neither had he any intention of frightening the poor little creature, so he took a few gentle paces backwards to help it feel less threatened.

After a minute or two, sensing no menace, it slowly uncurled — much to Yttrium's delight. His delight turned to mild alarm, however, when the hedgehog scurried towards him, its little nose twitching wildly. Suddenly, from out of nowhere, they were joined by three other hedgehogs, all with noses atwitch and heading straight for those feet.

Panic quickly set in and Yttrium took to his heels, running in ever increasing circles, with all four spiny quadrupeds in hot pursuit. Realising that it was getting nowhere fast, the oldest and wisest of their little number elected to stay put, on the assumption that all things come to he who waits — especially if those things are travelling in a circular direction — but Yttrium spotted the little beast in the nick of time.

Just as it was about to take a tasty bite from his foetid foot, Yttrium spun through 90 degrees, heading away from the pack as fast as he could. What he hadn't yet realised was that he was also heading, at quite a rate of knots now, away from his vehicle and safety.

After no more than twenty yards of pushing through the chin-high corn, his arms flailing in all directions and his lungs seeming fit to burst, he glanced over his shoulder to make sure they weren't gaining on him. Not a single hedgehog had followed his trail but, as he stood in sheer, thankful, amazement that they'd given up on their quarry, and wondering if it was safe to rush back to his vehicle, he could feel something nibbling at his toes.

"Now listen lads, not a word to the ol' bugger 'til 'ee'm sat down with 'is beer, right? No funny looks, no sniggerin', we don't want to give the game away, do us?" Georgie was at his best when he was scheming. He'd lain awake all night planning this little ruse, and wasn't about to have the cat let out of the bag — not until he was good and ready.

Word had spread like wildfire that he was up to something and, by lunchtime, the Shafton Arms was full. Everybody, it seemed, was in on the secret — everybody, that is, except Ned — who was now approaching the pub for his regular lunch time watering.

He should have known as soon as he entered that something was afoot. The place was never usually this busy at this time of day and, with so many people in the place, wasn't it just a touch unusual to be able to hear the old grandfather clock ticking in the corner? Such matters were of little consequence to Ned, his mind was on a far higher plane.

"Usual Ned?" enquired Georgie with a perfectly straight face — a dead giveaway on two counts had he but thought about it. For a start Ned never drank anything but Haymaker, from his customary quart mug, and secondly Georgie never, but never, had a straight face — not unless you tried to pass him a foreign coin while paying for a round. A few had tried over the years, only to see the thing immediately nailed to the wall for all to see. That, and the threat of seeing their goolies nailed up alongside it if they ever tried to pull such a stunt again, was enough to deter a repetition.

"Ar, an' make it snappy" retorted Ned, clearly impervious to the tell-tale signs that all was not as it might have been, as he perched himself on his bar stool — the only stool left vacant in a packed pub, with dozens of people standing.

Winking at Paddy O'Toole over by the light switches, Georgie gave the signal for the amusements to begin. As the lights flashed on and off, Ned began to notice that everyone was looking straight at him. Quickly checking to ensure he hadn't left his fly undone, which he assumed to be the reason for the flashing, he noticed a tall figure making his way through the crowd, bobbing up and down to avoid the imitation oak beams.

It was old Jack Marley, wearing a buttoned-up dentist's jacket and a face only the most seasoned of poker players could manage to hold. He was also sporting the most enormous pair of latex ears, left over from a Prince Charles look-alike contest, as he made a slow, but very deliberate bee-line for Ned.

Standing now full square in front of his old mate, and drawing himself to his full height, he reached out and removed Ned's moth-eaten old woollen cap, placed both hands on the shiny pate and closed his eyes — gently humming in monotone all the while.

When the humming stopped he opened his eyes and pronounced "'Tis life Jim, but not as we knows it. Better beam I up Scottie, afore they bleedin' klingons gets I."

At this the entire pub erupted in hoots of derision, and it was to be several hours before the old grandfather clock could, once again, make itself heard.

chapter 3

"What's up whack, is the pub shut, like, or what?" enquired Joss of his neighbour, over the garden fence. Ned chose to ignore him, preferring to dig his garden like fury.

Even Joss knew that serious digging was definitely not called for at this time of the year. A bit of hoeing, perhaps, to keep down the weeds from time to time, but all that heavy stuff with the spade was making him feel quite ill just watching. He also knew that if the Shafton Arms was open for business — as well as much of the time when it wasn't — Ned would be propping up the bar. Joss, however, was one of the few people not in the pub that lunchtime.

"'Ere, nobody 'aven't died like, 'ave they man?" he enquired, fearing he'd put his size nine in it yet again. "Lesley all right, is she?" he continued, looking around for signs of Ned's wife. He knew, as did everybody else in the village, that they were always arguing — the Thrubwells' was hardly a marriage made in heaven — but he wouldn't have gone as far as to .... Would he? Then why was he digging so furiously? It wasn't a hole he was digging, was it?

"Bloody 'ell, babe" he half-whispered, half screamed, as he raced into the kitchen, tripping over the doorstep and landing spread-eagled at Fleur's feet. Breathlessly he stuttered "'E's only gone an' ... soddin' well ... done it. Friggin' well ... flipped 'is ... flamin' lid this time 'asn't 'e?", trying to drag himself back up to his feet.

"Hey, cool it babe, like what's with all the drama? Who's gone and done what?"

"Old Ned, 'e's killed Lesley — look 'e's buryin' 'er in 'is garden " he half-shrieked, his need to make it a full shriek so dire his eyeballs were bulging out of their sockets, but he thought better of it. If Ned had gone this far he might easily turn on them too — once someone's brain goes addled they're likely to do all kinds of stupid things. Joss should know.

Following her husband out into the garden, stooping to avoid being seen over the fence, Fleur found a knot-hole in the larch lap and peered through. Joss, meanwhile, was crouched at her feet in a tight little ball, gazing anxiously up at his tall, willowy wife for signs of confirmation, and fearing the crazed recriminations of a mad man discovered.

"I don't like to say this, babe, but you'd better take a look at what I'm seeing" whispered Fleur intriguingly, "and you'd better brace yourself. Man, this is not a pretty sight." She was right.

Wearing an old, heavily stained, greasy apron over muddy corduroy trousers and a paint-splattered check shirt, and with hair that hadn't seen a comb for days, Lesley was sauntering down the garden path in her old, shabby, carpet slippers — the long ash of the cigarette in the corner of her mouth threatening to drop, any minute, into the mug of tea she was bringing out for Ned.

"'Ere 'ee are 'ee ol' bugger, and don't say I never does nothin' for 'ee" mumbled Lesley, the smoke from her cigarette irritating her eyes as she placed the mug on the path, beside Ned.

"Oh don't mention it, I'm sure, that's what I be 'ere for" she said sarcastically, turning to go back indoors as an unappreciative Ned continued digging furiously.

"Coo-ee, Lesley . . . it's only me" trilled Fleur, bobbing up like a demented Jack-in-the-box, with Joss scrambling madly to his feet wondering what the hell was going on.

"I was wondering how you were, like, only I haven't bumped into you for a while — er, keeping alright are you?" she politely enquired, casting a glance in Joss' direction as Lesley hurriedly removed her apron, smoothed down her hair, and headed towards her neighbours.

"I be alright, ta very much, 'tis that miserable ol' bleeder over yonder. 'Aven't said so much as a dicky bird all afternoon, not sin' 'e got back from the pub. Still, serves 'im right, dunnit? Always takin' the piss out of others, but don't like it when they takes it out of 'e, do 'e?". Lesley regaled the incredulous pair with the events of the last twenty-four hours, at least how she saw them, and left them in no doubt that Ned had, finally, gone to play with the fairies.

Drastic situations call for drastic actions, and action men like Joss don't need telling twice when the chips are down. His old mate was in need of a friend, and if he couldn't go and enjoy his beer in peace, then his peace-inducing beer must go to him.

Drawing a couple of pints of his home-made, somewhat specialist and highly potent ale, Joss carried them carefully next door and out into the garden, where Ned was close to exhaustion — still digging away for all he was worth.

"Thought you might be ready for a livener, whack,

summink to put a bit of lead in yer pencil like" grinned Joss, proffering a pint mug in Ned's direction while taking a hefty slurp from his own.

Now mugs of tea, or even friendly greetings, could be easily ignored when Ned was in his blackest of moods — but beer? He was always brought up to be polite to anyone who gives you beer, and this was no time to start changing the habits of a lifetime.

"That's real 'andsome of 'ee, whacker me ol' mate, don't mind if I do" he responded cheerily, if a little out of breath, "don't mind if I do at all".

A pint in Ned's hands is not something you would bet on breaking longevity records, especially with an hour's digging behind him and a serious thirst to quench, but he had the utmost respect for Joss' ale. That its potency owed more to the Shafton Rose than to the meer fermentation of yeast, sugar, and malted barley, there could be little doubt, but for its chemical composition he cared not a jot. He was in serious need of a little oblivion right now.

As the awful, embarrassing, events at the Shafton Arms receded to the back of his mind at last, he was left with the most vivid impression of his experience at Farthing Fflitch. His self-confidence also returned, sufficiently for him to be able to blurt out the entire story to Joss who, unlike Georgie, was prepared to keep an open mind. An open mind was always one of Joss' strengths, but then there was rarely enough in it to warrant keeping it closed anyway.

"Do 'ee want for I to take 'ee ther?" offered Ned, somewhat emboldened by his friend's interest.

"Yeah, yer on whack" smiled Joss, "real groovy man, only me van's off the road, like, needin' some major surgery, so we'll have to leg it."

"Nar, bain't no problem ther me ol' sonner, 'ee leave

it to ol' Ned. Gravy man, like far in."

Half an hour later, with Joss balancing precariously on the crossbar of Ned's bike, the pair were free-wheeling down the narrow, leafy lane approaching Farthing Fflitch. As he dismounted at the pre-ordained spot, Joss had thoughts for little else other than that part of his anatomy which had been caressing the crossbar.

So numb was it by now that the stinging nettles, into which he tumbled when his legs gave way, had absolutely no effect — which was just as well as Ned didn't relish the thought of applying the dock leaf antidote. It's at times like this you realise just who your true friends are.

Ned remembered the spot well — he wasn't likely to forget it in a hurry — and could even point to the skid marks left on the lane by his bike's tyres. What he couldn't point to, however, was the spaceship. It had gone, and with it, it seemed, had his credibility.

He was now having serious doubts about just what he'd seen — or thought he'd seen — as he scrambled through the hedge looking for evidence of its existence. Was he losing his marbles, as everyone thought? Joss would have none of it, however. If Ned said he'd seen a spaceship, then a spaceship it must have been, and there must be some tell-tale signs that it had been here. Besides, he didn't much fancy the return journey just yet, despite the awful stench in the air around these parts.

The vehicle had been moved from the corn field, of course, which is why the intrepid alien hunters hadn't spotted it. Argona had been awoken from her deep slumber by Yttrium's panic, coming under attack, as he had, by further curious hedgehogs.

By the time she'd realised what was going on and

brought the vehicle overhead, all she could see was Yttrium scrambling through the base jelly, half a dozen demented, spiky Earth creatures scurrying around, and three neat circles — a large one at each end joined to the smaller, central circle, by a completely straight line.

Where the vehicle had stood, however, the corn was completely unbowed. The base jelly had been well designed, and was sufficiently compliant to shape itself perfectly to its surroundings — creating, in the process, an almost perfect vacuum which would anchor the vehicle in position.

Entirely surrounded by the jelly, each individual ear of corn — although fully matured and awaiting harvest — had succumbed to energy fields of immense power and, in a few short hours, had doubled in both size and weight. Ned was the first to spot the anomaly.

"Over yer, whacker me ol' mate, what's think of 'e then?" he yelled, "look, 'tis a ruddy girt circle of the stuff — so 'ow do 'ee explain that then, eh?"

"Wow, man, like far out. But 'old on a sec, whack, could be a reason for it, like". He racked his poor little brain, desperately seeking some kind of logical answer to the strange concept with which it was now being presented, and eventually surprised himself with what he came up with.

"Got it" he smiled proudly, "what if the farmer bloke only 'ad enough fertiliser to do this bit, like?" he concluded, feeling more like Sherlock Holmes with every passing second. He was even moved to venture "Elementary, dear Whatsit" as he polished his grubby little finger nails on his kaftan.

"Oh ar, so 'e just dumps it like, in a perfect bleedin' circle, right in the middle of 'is field do 'e? 'Ow'd 'e do that then, with a bleedin' 'elicopter? An what 'bout they then?" he posed, pointing to Yttrium's circles.

Joss had to admit that there he was stumped. Who in their right mind would want to flatten perfectly good corn? It didn't make any sense. And they were perfect circles, and perfectly aligned. The only possible explanation was that Ned's spaceship had been here after all and left a calling card — but what could it possibly mean?

Well the crew at the Shafton Arms were going to have to eat their words right enough, but first port of call would have to be Ron Runstable, the village bobby. He'd certainly want to let the Prime Minister know personally — you couldn't just have illegal immigrants coming into the country as they pleased, no matter where they came from, I mean, where would it all end?

As the excited pair mounted Ned's rusty old bike — at times like this he really could do with the other two gears — they were completely unaware of the eyes following their every move. The small, piggy, pink-tinged eyes peered over the six digits of the pale, sallow left hand which parted the hedgerow, while the huge, deep purple, eyes gazed over the six digits of both green hands which parted the corn.

So, thought Yttrium, the spiky little quadrupeds are not the only form of life, they also have bipeds. Quite advanced as well, thought Argona, they've even discovered the wheel apparently — but I'm sure they could do more with it if they really applied themselves, she mused, watching Ned struggle back up the lane while Joss massaged his aching, stinging, backside.

I believe they've come much further than we give them credit for you know, my dear, suggested Yttrium. Whilst going through my pre-disembarkation checks last night, I actually picked up a number of radio frequencies in use. Now unless they're naturally occurring emissions that, surely, would suggest signs of intelligent life, would it not?

Right then Mr Know-it-all, fumed Argona, angry at herself for failing to spot the frequencies, tune us into one of your 'intelligent life-form' signals — if you can. Concentrating very hard on the frequency range in question, he stumbled across the output of a heavy rock radio station and, for a full minute, their delicately balanced little minds were blown completely.

Rapidly moving off frequency to kill the cacophonous assault on their senses, Yttrium had to agree that no intelligent life form would want to create such a racket deliberately. It therefore had to be either a naturally-occurring signal, or some kind of tribal warfare. Maybe the biped beings used it to blast each other off their two-wheeled machines, he pondered, but Argona had grown quite fond of it.

Scanning through the airwaves once more, he came across a bunch of signals which appeared to generate visual images as well — and homed in on one to investigate further. Flickering a little at first, until he was able to fine tune it, the signal eventually came through loud and clear, so he phased Argona into the same frequency.

"Well I'm telling you now, lady, yon lad's nobutta cheeky little begga" said the biped with red hair, looking angry, "and if he doesn't buck his ideas up, he's for the sack, and no mistake. What do you reckon?"

"Well, I don't really know, Rita" whined the grey-haired biped, clearly a subordinate of the other from her very posture, "does that mean Derek'll have to deliver the papers tomorrow morning, or what?"

And that's intelligent life? thought Argona.

Ron Runstable had just sat down to his favourite dinner, steak and kidney pud with lashings of thick, meaty gravy — as only Ruby could make it — with a veritable pile of mashed potato, and cabbage fresh from his allotment. The familiar strains of the signature tune on the telly, in the front room, signalled the end of 'Coronation Street', which meant that Ruby would soon be up and about preparing his treacle pudding for afters. What more could a man ask for?

"Well 'e's 'avin' 'is dinner right now, can you come back in 'alf an 'our?" reached Runstable's finely tuned hearing organs. You didn't get to be a pillar of society if you didn't have finely tuned hearing organs, and used them to earwig at every possible opportunity.

"Is that what Churchill said to 'itler when 'e were gunna invade — 'Can you come back in 'alf 'our when we've 'ad our dinner ?' Out of my way woman, 'tis important business I've come about, wer's 'e to?" insisted Ned, forcing his way past Ruby, with a suitably embarrassed Joss in his wake.

"Nar then, nar then, what's all this commotion about" yelled the rotund copper, more than just a little upset at Ned's sense of timing. He had no objection to coitus interruptus, provided that the interruption was on genuine Police business, and didn't really mind being disturbed in the lavatory, if it was urgent. You could even call him away from his pint of beer if you really had to, but steak and kidney pudding was quite a different matter.

"They buggers was laughin' at I down the pub this dinner time" started Ned, not really quite sure just where to begin with his report.

"An' you come bargin' in yer, spoilin' me dinner to tell I that? They'm always laughin' at 'ee down the pub, 'ee dafty ol' git, now bugger off out of it — afore I run 'ee in for wastin' Police time".

"No, listen, 'tis important — 'ee dinner can wait 'ee fat ol' sod" continued Ned, completely unperturbed, "ther's a bleedin' spaceship landed down Farthin' Fflitch

— come an' see for 'ee self if 'ee don't believe I".

How sad, thought the old constable, that it should come to this. He and Ned went way back, probably longer than either of them cared to think about, and all that time he'd been warning his friend about the dangers of excessive alcohol abuse. And now the pigeons had finally come home to roost.

The constant, eager, head bobbing agreement from his companion didn't cut much ice either, standing there like Noddy on heat — everyone knew he was a dope head, just couldn't prove it that's all. What the hell was Runstable to do now — his dinner was going colder by the minute.

"Now why don't 'ee come 'long with I, me ol' mucker, an' 'ave a nice chat with Doctor Foster. An' as fer 'ee" said Runstable sternly to the hippy vision affronting his senses, "I'll be 'avin' words with 'ee later. Now clear off 'ome wer 'ee belongs."

"But we gotta tell the guv'ment" insisted Ned, "ther could be more of they things on the way for all we knows, come to take us over like, could even be lookin' for folks to do speriments on."

"Well they can 'ave 'ee ther for a start" laughed Runstable, nodding in Joss' direction, "that ought to make sure the buggers don't come back again." He quite appreciated the wit he could muster in such trying circumstances — what with his dinner going cold and all — but decided not to push his luck too far. Quit while you're ahead, my old son, he thought to himself.

"Now come an' jump in the panda car with I, Ned, an' I'll take 'ee to see the doc" he coaxed softly, not wishing to unbalance the poor old soul further, "an' flower power 'ere'll take 'ee bike 'ome fer 'ee, won't 'ee son?"

"Look 'ere 'ee cloth-eared ol' bugger, bain't nothin' wrong with I, 'cept for I can't get through to 'ee, so stop goin' on 'bout the bleedin' doctor an' get 'ee arse in gear for Gawd's sake — afore 'tis too soddin' late!" Ned was becoming just a little impatient.

"Alright, tell 'ee what I be gunna do" conceded Runstable, "If I phones through to 'ampton and reports a UFO, an' then asks if ther's bin any other reports in the area, us'll know if anybody else seen it, 'on't us?"

"Listen 'ee soppy tart, if anybody else seen it we'd 'ave all 'eared 'bout it by now — only 'ee 'ouldn't be laughin' at they an' wantin' to take they to the doc's 'ould 'ee? Now get that bleedin' car of yorn out, an' let's get goin'."

"To the doc's?"

"To Farthin' Fflitch."

Runstable knew when he was beaten. You didn't get to be a well respected upholder of the Law without knowing when you was beaten — besides, he'd be back in half an hour, Ned and the dropout would have been silenced, and he could then get on with his warmed up dinner in peace.

Stifling a yawn as he carefully threaded the panda car through the narrow lane, hoping he wouldn't have to go as far as Frankie's cattle grid, Runstable could think of little else but his beautiful steak and kidney pud — with all that lovely gravy just drying up in the oven. Crying shame.

"'Twas roun' yer somewhere" declared Ned semi-confidently, although the failing light was taking its toll on his memory, "mebbe just roun' the next bend?" he ventured.

"'Tis 'ee 'oo be drivin' I roun' the bend" declared the hungry bobby, his stomach suffering torment for which it was never designed. If he didn't get to eat soon he was likely to pass out from sheer malnutrition.

"Stop yer" screamed Ned, his pot-bellied, sweet-toking

cohort nodding full agreement. He had no idea why he was agreeing, but if Ned was screaming he must be on to something.

"Over there, man, to your right" yelled Joss, suddenly spotting it, "now is that cool, or what, like?"

"'Oly shite!" declared the incredulous copper, as the unmistakeable green glow of the vehicle hove into view from behind the small copse.

Steak and kidney pud was off tonight.

chapter 4

"Oh, Mr Stick" called out the secretary, just as Joss was trying to sneak back in unnoticed from his extended lunch break, "Lady Prosser would like to see you please, at 4.30 in the Managing Director's office."

"But I'm only ten minutes late . . ." he started to reply, but to no avail, she had already gone into the ladies'.

Well, this is it, he realised, it's the sack for me. To be fair, Lady Prosser hadn't let any of the workforce go during these troubled times but, with her son languishing at Her Majesty's pleasure, the business couldn't be expected to last for ever.

Joss had only had to make three pairs of plastic gonads this week which, even allowing for the considerable warming-up period his injection moulding machine required, only kept him busy for a couple of hours. The rest of the time was spent reading the paper, drinking mugs of tea and coffee, and staring aimlessly out of the window at the car park. Not much of a life, admittedly, but at least it paid the bills — or it did until 4.30 this afternoon.

There wasn't even much social chit-chat to occupy his time, as his machine was in a separate room — arranged by Prosser to keep prying eyes away from the hollow testes required for his drug running. Joss had also been given Foreman status by Prosser, thereby eliminating the involvement of the Workshop Foreman in this little sideline. It also meant his former workmates were less inclined to chat with him, so even his coffee breaks were lonely occasions.

The only human contact he got during the day was with his wife, Fleur, when he went home for lunch — just two minutes walk away, the other side of the car park. Understandably, perhaps, he'd been stretching his lunch breaks these last few weeks, but now it appeared he'd been found out and would have to pay the penalty.

Throughout that long afternoon, with no gentlemen's accessories to make, and with his machine and floor space sparkling from the cleaning and polishing he'd been occupying himself with, he had little to do other than mentally rehearse what he was going to say to Lady Prosser at 4.30.

Perhaps she would listen to reason and find some other way to punish his tardiness. Maybe she could be persuaded to demote him — yes, he'd like that. He'd be able to talk to his workmates again, that would help to pass the time of day. Perhaps if he begged her to keep him on, but no, he realised in his heart of hearts that the axe was about to fall. Why else would she call for him at that time of day, just as everybody was going home?

With Mickey Mouse's left hand now well past his right, and rapidly approaching Donald Duck, Joss brushed his clean, flower-bedecked, bell-bottomed overalls, straightened his floral motif kipper tie, and made his way up the stairs to hear his fate. He had but one thing on his mind — how the hell was he going to break the news to Fleur?

The Workshop Foreman was just leaving the office as Joss reached the top of the stairs, the overpowering stench of his armpits causing Joss to heave. This was one feature of Prossers he would certainly not miss. The Foreman cast a most evil glance in his direction, indicating perhaps that he'd been consulted about Joss' departure.

He couldn't expect any support from that quarter, that's for sure so, prepared for the worst, he rapped on the door of the Acting Managing Director of Prosser Prosthetics Plc.

"An' I be tellin' 'ee, Sarge, I knows what I saw — an' I 'ad two witnesses ... No I 'ad not been drinkin', I 'ouldn't 'ave been drivin' else ... Yes, Sarge, I'll be ther in 'alf an 'our." Runstable replaced the receiver on its cradle, on his little wooden desk, in his tiny village Police Station, and wiped his profusely sweating hands on the front of his tunic.

Two men from the Ministry of Defence were waiting to interview him over at Hampton Magna, alerted by the report he'd submitted last night. The new duty Sergeant had refused to accept his verbal report — said it made no sense at all and that Runstable must be off his rocker — and insisted on a full written report, in triplicate, before he'd pass it up the line.

The new Sergeant, Steve Roberts, wasn't a bad bloke at all, far less abrasive than Sergeant Argent — whose departure from The Hampshire Constabulary had been unusually swift. 'Hushed up' was the phrase on everybody's lips, indicating that top brass had come to some kind of arrangement with Argent, although the lads couldn't understand why Ron Runstable seemed so smug about it all.

But Sergeant Roberts hadn't been in the job long enough to feel secure, and on receiving Runstable's initial, almost incoherent, report, had insisted on getting it in writing simply to cover his own back. If one of his lads wanted to put in a report like that then fine, on his own head be it, but Roberts wasn't about to join him in the funny farm.

That Runstable was a touch nervous about the forthcoming ordeal was understandable — it's not every day you see a spaceship and then have to convince others. But he was as certain as he could be about the terrible apparition — here, hang about, he thought, couldn't have been one of they mirages could it? Like they gets in the desert. No, couldn't possibly be, there wasn't any sand for miles around, and it was definitely sand that caused mirages, because they were only seen in the desert.

Round and around spun his mind, as he drove to Hampton, trying to find logical alternative explanations for what he'd clearly experienced. You could be certain the Ministry of Defence wallahs would be questioning him, very closely indeed, so it paid to think things through beforehand.

"And these witnesses of yours, constable?" asked the boffin, peering down at Runstable's written report which lay before him, " a Mr Stick and a Mr Thrubwell, is that correct?"

"Ar, Joss an' Ned. Good lads, the pair of 'em, honest as the day is long, sir."

"Quite. But are they not both, er, shall we say, known to the Police for certain activities? Thrubwell, I believe, was held in this very room on suspicion of drugs dealing, and not all that long ago — am I right constable?"

"Well, sort of — but 'twas all a terrible misunderstandin', sir. Turned out 'e 'ad no idea what it was 'e were sellin' at the W I Jumble Sale."

"Shafton Roses, I believe he called them, sir" chipped in Sergeant Roberts, trying to be helpful.

"Indeed? And this fellow Stick, wasn't he suspected of cultivating these 'Shafton Roses'? And isn't he also known to your colleagues in Liverpool, constable?"

"Well I do believe 'e 'ad a bit of bother a few years back, sir, but 'tis all behind 'im now."

"I see. 'Good lads, the pair of them, and honest as the day is long.' eh?" said the boffin slowly, with just the teensiest touch of sarcasm, clearly intended to impress his older, but as yet silent, colleague sitting in the corner, taking it all in.

"These 'good lads' of yours weren't smoking anything on your drive to Farthing Fflitch were they? Something which you, too, may have inhaled — oh, passively, of course — in the close confines of a Police car?"

"No, sir, not so much as a Woodbine, sir. Nobody don't smoke nothin' in my car, sir, nor in my station, sir, er, beggin' your pardon, sir." He shuffled nervously on his seat as the boffin lit his pipe.

"So then, to what do you attribute the illusion you reported, constable, er, Runstable, isn't it?" he posed, trying to read his notes through the thick smoke now belching forth from his mouth, his nose and, imagined Runstable, every other conceivable orifice.

"Weren't no 'lusion, sir, I knows what I seen."

"And just what was it that you seen — er, saw?"

"All ther in my report, sir." replied Runstable matter of factly, although sounding just a touch imperious. "Oh, er, beggin' your pardon, sir," he continued, realising that trying to be a smartarse was unlikely to win him any brownie points, "what it was, was a girt big green spaceship, sir, proceedin' very slowly in a northeasterly direction, 'bout a 'undred foot off the ground."

"I see. And what made you think it was a spaceship? Were there, for example, spacemen — or, perhaps, to be more politically correct, spacepersons — on board?"

"Couldn't say, sir, didn't 'ang around to find out. Ther was summat odd 'bout it though, sir, it didn't make no noise. Silent as the grave it were. An' it glowed, this strange kind of eerie green glow, like one of they luminous watches on a dark night." Runstable was waxing lyrical.

"An' in my report, sir" he continued, "you'll see that Mr Thrubwell an' Mr Stick mentioned some curious things 'bout the corn crop in the field. Now I ain't seen it meself, like, not yet, but it do sound a bit weird, don't it?"

"We'll be investigating that in due course, constable. Probably find a logical explanation for it — we usually do — but in the meanwhile you're to treat the entire matter as an Official Secret, as defined in paragraph 27, clause 14 of the Official Secrets Act. I'm sure I don't need to remind you of the consequences of any breaches of said Act. Do you understand?"

With that he was dismissed to return to his duties and, as he left the room, his every move was observed very closely by the elderly, quiet gentleman in the corner.

"Please come in Mr Stick, so sorry to have kept you waiting" apologised Lady Prosser, "do, please, take a seat." This was a first for Joss, he'd never been fired sitting down before. He usually stood to attention as he was being given the boot — quite why he never really knew, it just seemed the right thing to do.

"I'll come straight to the point, Mr Stick. You will be aware that this company is going through something of a crisis at the moment. I am doing my level best to keep the ship afloat but, to be perfectly frank, I lack both the managerial and the entrepreneurial skills required. I am also, I'm afraid, far too long in the tooth to start learning" she smiled.

Joss was beginning to warm to the old bird. She was, without a shadow of a doubt, by far the nicest person ever to have fired him. He was even beginning to feel sorry he was leaving.

"It was the late Sir Paul's policy" she continued, "and one which stood this company in very good stead, to always promote from within. I have, as you probably realise, already discussed this with the Workshop Foreman, Mr Grungemould, and now it's your turn.

"I would like you to come up with ideas for turning around the fortunes of this company, and Mr Grungemould is doing the same. You may, if you wish, present your ideas in the form of a business plan — something those dreadful people at the bank keep insisting on — but in any event I need something from you by the end of next week.

"And don't feel hemmed in by traditional thinking. New ideas, lateral thinking, those were the tenets Sir Paul founded this business on, and that's what is required to get us out of this mess, am I making myself clear?"

Joss' ears had heard every word she'd said, and many of them had filtered through into his brain, but it was his mouth he was having difficulty with. It just flapped about, making not a sound.

"Are you alright, Mr Stick? Not feeling unwell are you? Oh dear, I hope all this hasn't come as too much of a shock to you, it was foolish of me to suddenly spring it on you like that, please forgive me."

"No, your Honour, er, I mean, your Lady" blurted Joss.

"Emilia" interjected Lady Prosser. "Sir Paul was always known to his employees simply as Paul, even after his knighthood, and that is a tradition I should very much like to continue. After all, if Jesus could be addressed by his Christian name, who are we to hide behind titles?"

"No, er, Emilia" continued Joss, beginning to feel a little less uncomfortable but still somewhat incredulous, "no, I'm feelin' fine, like, only I was expectin' the sack, man, er, I mean, Emilia."

"The sack? Good gracious alive. I've never sacked anybody in my life and I don't intend to start now. No, if we go down, we all go down together — but we are not going down without a fight. Do you get my drift, man" she smiled benignly.

Joss still couldn't believe what was happening. Here he was, in the boss' office, being consulted on what could only be described as the making or breaking of the company, by a Lady who was treating him as her equal. Fleur wasn't going to believe it either.

"Of course, you do realise you are in competition with Mr Grungemould, don't you? A little competition never hurt anybody, Sir Paul always believed it brought out the best in a man. And you'll not find me ungenerous when the appointment is decided."

"Appointment?"

"Of course. Whoever is deemed to have come up with the brightest ideas will be given every opportunity to make them work. The job title, initially, will be Manager — but make no mistake, if it's a success then a seat on the Board will follow."

'Business Plans','Lateral Thinking','Seat On The Board', what on earth was happening to him? He didn't know whether to laugh or cry — he couldn't even decide whether to rush straight home and tell Fleur, or to try and get it straight in his mind first and then tell her.

"Well then, Sergeant," mused the boffin, looking up

from his notes, "and just what do you make of this nonsense, eh?"

"Not for me to say sir," replied Sergeant Roberts, "I merely passed the report up the line as required, it was Winchester who called you lot in. Do you turn out for all these jobs then, I mean, you must get hundreds of these UFO reports, or is there something special about this one?"

"I'm sure you wouldn't expect me to answer questions relating to MOD procedure, Sergeant, suffice it to say that I am interested enough to be here. Now, if you would be so kind, perhaps you would take us to this Farthing Ffitch place" he replied sternly.

"Fflitch" came a response from the corner, the first word his mysterious colleague had uttered since his arrival, "It's Farthing Fflitch."

Neither did he make any further utterances on the journey to the corn field, he just sat in the back of the Police Range Rover watching the world go by. He was, however, watching very intently, and even reached for his notebook when they crossed the ford at Hatch End, noting with interest the height of the swollen river.

Arriving at the spot marked by Ned's bike tyres and, a few feet further on, Runstables car tyres, the Sergeant turned on his hazard warning lights, together with his blue roof mounted light so that the parked car could be clearly seen above the hedgerow. It certainly was.

Leading the way through the gap in the hedge with Roberts right behind him, the boffin held a handkerchief to his face to try and filter out the appalling smell. Neither was Roberts too enamoured with the odour. He'd had to put up with worse in his career — not much worse, it's true — but it's all part of the job. He was far less pleased with the rip in his tunic, caught on a blackthorn as he forced his way through the hedge.

The other man continued down the lane for about thirty yards, to Frankie's cattle grid, then gained access to the field by way of a five barred gate. He seemed not to notice the smell.

The look on the younger boffin's faced changed quite dramatically, from a mixture of repulsion tinged with tedium to one of sheer disbelief when he came upon the circles — he even dropped his handkerchief. He'd seen dozens of the things before of course and, without exception, he'd been able to demonstrate how the hoaxers had created their little masterpieces.

The one thing which gave them all away was the need to get amongst the standing corn — without flattening any unintentionally. They usually followed wheel tracks, left by huge modern farm machinery — but here there were none. Failing that they would tiptoe carefully through the crop, carrying their implements aloft, but it was impossible to do that without flattening at least a few stalks along the way. Here the field was in pristine condition, despite the recent heavy rain and winds.

The variety planted was one of the older strains, shorter and thicker in the stalk but yielding less corn to the acre. It was, however, more resistant to the diseases to which many of the modern hybrids fall prey. To counteract the low yield, the farmer had sown his seed more thickly, providing plenty of fertiliser — the source of which was pretty obvious from the stench — and it would be impossible to walk across such a field without leaving any trace.

But when he stumbled across the huge circle of enlarged corn ears, as mentioned in Runstable's report, he was totally incredulous. There could be no logical explanation for this either. The only way additional fertiliser could be delivered to just one part of the field would be by high pressure spray, and there was just no way a perfect circle could be achieved by that method.

Neither would additional fertiliser produce such a startling addition to the yield — not even the highly potent mess this bloke had obviously used — it just didn't stack up, didn't stack up at all.

There had to be an explanation of course, you can't just have MOD files slopping around in the system with question marks all over them, that would never do. He would have to call in the heavy mob, armed to the teeth with equipment to measure everything which could be measured. They'd then feed all the data into one or more of their computer programmes, compare it with data from other circle hoaxes, and eventually come up with the answer.

Why they had to go to all this time and trouble, just because some practical joker had found a different way of playing this little game, was beyond him. You learned not to question orders at the MOD however — it could lead to a major career adjustment. When the big cheese said jump, the only question one could legitimately raise — and then only very tactfully — was the altitude one was required to achieve.

That wouldn't be necessary on this occasion, however, because the big cheese was right here with him — watching his every move. Without a second thought for the further damage he may be doing to the farmer's crop, the older man waded straight into the middle of the field, noting how the flattened corn was laid in just one direction.

Nothing unusual there, that was pretty much par for the course, but it was the simplicity of the pattern which intrigued him. Of late the hoaxes had become quite intricate, almost grotesque, but this had a simplicity seemingly intended to leave as clear a message as possible. Just what the message was, and who the messenger may be, remained to be answered.

He returned to his two companions, carrying two normal ears of corn in his right hand and two of the enlarged ears in his left. Although he was no agricultural expert, Sergeant Roberts was intrigued by the difference.

He was even more intrigued, however, by the six digits on the man's left hand.

chapter 5

Whilst the MOD men had seen, at first hand, the circles left behind by our alien friends, and would undoubtedly gather much more information from the site, as yet they had not found any conclusive evidence that the phenomenon was of extraterrestrial origin.

Neither was there any evidence of hoaxers having been on the site. The fact that in the previous eight or nine years some three thousand crop circle events had been recorded, might just have caused the younger boffin to suspect a more earthly explanation. But the one thing which would have opened his mind a little, sight of the vehicle itself, had eluded him — for the time being.

By now it was well out of sight, our inter-galactic gypsies having decided to find long-term parking for it. They were quite certain their presence here had been detected and, as they had first and foremost to find food suitable to concentrate before recommencing their travels, they would have to remain here a while longer. Besides, it would soon be Argona's birthday, and this did seem rather a nice place to celebrate it.

Whilst they had experienced nothing, as yet, to suggest a hostile reception if they were to make contact with the bipeds, Yttrium was quite convinced they were a warlike lot — why else would they want to blast each other off their two-wheeled machines with those infernal radio signals? Better to be safe than sorry and, as the vehicle was the most visible element of their existence, the sooner it was out of sight the better.

Bearing in mind the need to protect the plasma jelly from drying out, the river offered the safest storage facility. The manoeuvrability of such a craft is pretty good, the skilled exponent only has to think what is required and the vehicle complies. It's a little like the concept of virtual reality — without the virtual.

It's not even necessary to be inside the thing in order to control it which is just as well because, when super density mode is called for, it can get a touch cramped inside. This is the mode used for long-term garaging on Strontium, without it you simply wouldn't be able to move for vehicles parked all over the place, but it was now proving extremely useful for concealment purposes.

The entire vehicle, at the extreme of the modal spectrum, would compact down to a size no bigger than a football — except that it remained flat at the bottom to spread its not inconsiderable weight as evenly as possible, bearing in mind that just a teaspoonful of super dense plasma jelly weighs half a ton in earth's gravity.

To have something that heavy simply dropping into a river from a very great height might just have attracted a little attention so, standing on the river bank, a mile or so upstream from the primitive dwellings of the bipeds of Farthing Fflitch in the dead of night, Argona gradually adjusted the density — and thus, in direct proportion, the size of the vehicle — as it was gently lowered into the river.

When it reached the river bed, about six feet below the surface of the fast flowing water, its sheer weight held it steadier than any rock these waters had ever tried to shift. Gravel very quickly built up around the vehicle and, with all but its essential maintenance systems de-activated, the eerie green glow diminished to a deep green sheen, matching perfectly the weeds which surrounded it.

As a final touch Argona lightened the density of several dozen, well chosen, tiny, strands of plasma and allowed them to string out several feet as they gently swung, to and fro, in the current.

Now that's just showing off, thought Yttrium loudly, clearly impressed with his partner's handiwork but not wanting her to know it — he'd never live it down. And with that little job now taken care of, they set off into the night, hand in hand, in search of plant materials which might prove edible.

Their activities had not gone unnoticed, however, but then nothing in Farthing Fflitch ever did. The populace may not be all that great in number, nor indeed in terms of the I Q they could rustle up between them on a good day, but they certainly knew when there were strangers about.

The sound of the approaching Police car's engine had awoken Frankie Fflitch and, long before he'd seen the blue light, he was in his Land Rover and about to set off for the cattle grid, the palm of his ready cupped left hand itching like fury. He'd thought better of it on spotting the light though, and instead made his way stealthily on foot to find out what was going on.

He was joined, within minutes, by half a dozen other assorted members of the clan Fflitch, all eager for excitement as the silent, single-file procession made its way along the hedgerow and up into the huge boughs of the old oak tree overlooking the cornfield. There they'd watched, totally perplexed, as a Policeman and two other blokes searched the field — but for what? Corn? Is that what they'd come for, two handfuls of sodding corn?

Frankie had been the only witness of the previous evening's visitors, but had at least been entertained as the pot-bellied hippy buffoon tumbled into the nettles, but this lot were just boring. All they did was wander about the field, speaking in very low voices which was so frustrating.

Poor old Fenella, a wretched, toothless crone in her sixty third year — as far as anyone could work out — had become so tired of the proceedings that she almost fell asleep, and out of the tree. The only thing keeping her awake was cousin Frederick's trick of sticking his big toe up his nose. Fenella had grown so fond of that trick over the years, and of course there was nothing Frederick liked better than an appreciative audience.

But at least the visitors, however unwelcome they may be, provided a break from the tedium of life in the remote hamlet. There was only one television in the entire community, an old black and white crystal valve set dumped by some outsider who couldn't be bothered taking it to the tip. On dark winter evenings, when there was absolutely nothing else to do, there would be anything up to a couple of dozen Fflitches gathered around that old set, totally intrigued by it.

Frankie was the only one allowed to play with the knobs as he was the technically-minded one, anybody else would undoubtedly break it, but the interesting thing was the pecking order of seating arrangements. The oldest members of the clan — those with failing eyesight — would sit on the floor, just a few feet from the telly, resting their backs against the legs of the young parents sat on the wooden chairs, holding their youngsters so that they, too, could marvel at this modern innovation.

Behind them would stand the macho young men, it being a matter of great pride among them to see who could stand perfectly still, on one spot, the longest. Skills like that don't come naturally, they have to be worked at over many years of standing perfectly still, on one spot, and only when those skills had been honed to perfection could one claim one's place on the back row. Until that time youngsters had to suffer the indignity of being hung from the rafters, by the breeches, along with the other kids, when watching the telly.

All in all, telly gatherings were a sight to behold, one which any anthropologist worth his salt would give his eye teeth to study. And it will become even more fascinating if they ever get electricity in Farthing Fflitch.

Long after the Police car had reversed back up the lane, and the audience had descended from their tree and made their way home, several of them had been awoken by the strange, eerie green light which passed silently overhead and down the river. This wasn't the first time they'd been pestered by hot air balloonists, but Frankie was determined to ensure it was the last.

Grabbing his shot gun he'd raced out into the night, tripped over Fenella who was crouched up in a tight ball on the floor, fearing it was a big bird that might shit on her, and fell headlong into the river. By the time he'd got enough mud and grit out of the barrels to be able to force the cartridges in, the bloody thing had disappeared, much to his annoyance, but he'd vowed to have the next bastard that tried to fly over Farthing Fflitch.

"I want the entire area cordoned off, orders from upstairs" said the young boffin over his steaming hot cup of MOD tea, "and a complete news blackout until we've bottomed this one. We don't want Joe Public crawling all over the place, not until we've collected all the data for analysis, do I make myself clear?"

"Yes sir, perfectly, but where am I going to get the resources required for such a task?" enquired Inspector Hector on the other end of the phone. "Overtime for this month is already way over quota, and I'm understaffed as it is — can't the MOD Police help?"

"Certainly not Richard, I'm not having those flat-footed, cauliflower-eared apes down there. Besides, we want to keep this as low-profile as possible. Local bobbies will also know the lie of the land, who owns what, and all that kind of thing — so just make sure you send enough men to do the job properly. Where you get them from is your problem — just make sure you get them."

"Sergeant Roberts, get Runstable on the blower for me would you, immediately please" yelled the frustrated Inspector. He really needed this right now. He'd had three PC's leave in the last month, frustrated at the lack of overtime and their inability to meet their mortgage payments without it, on top of which Winchester had now told him he couldn't replace them — not for the foreseeable future at least — and all the time his crime figures were mounting steadily.

And to cap it all he'd had to sort out that sordid business with Sergeant Argent. That had turned out to be a blessing in disguise, as indeed had Argent, because he couldn't stand the bloke. Neither could his PC's so it was just as well the Met had agreed to take him back. Following a short period of hospitalisation, WPC Argent was now once again dishing out parking tickets down the Mile End Road.

"Bloody fine can of worms you've opened up here, Runstable, and no mistake. Now look, what's the minimum number of blokes you'll need for 24 hour surveillance on that sodding corn field of yours? There's to be nobody in and nobody out without a pass, and the whole area's got to be kept absolutely secure until the MOD wallahs have finished. So how many do you reckon, two enough?"

"That'll be 'nough for one end of the lane alright, sir, but ther's t'other end to think 'bout, an' the river, then ther's 'undreds of ways in across the fields like. Reckon I be gunna need 'bout forty or fifty, then treble that for shifts roun' the clock. Could do with a dozen or so of they 'orseback lads, 'alf a dozen dog 'andlers — oh, an' a 'elicopter for I to oversee it all like."

"Dream on Runstable, you'll have three PC's and like it. I'm giving you the three newest lads — hopefully they'll be keen enough to want to impress, get some sort of commendation on their record. It's the least I can do for them, because there's no paid overtime on this job."

"Do that include I, sir?"

"Especially you, Runstable, it was your damned report that started all this fiasco and don't you forget it! Now get over to Farthing Fflitch and set up your road blocks."

Runstable wasn't sure whether to laugh or cry. On the one hand he was definitely in charge of this job, with three rookies at his beck and call, and it was about time his years of service were recognised. But on the other hand it meant he'd be working around the clock, unable to go home for his dinner — and what was he going to do when he needed to use the lavatory? His logistical problems were only just beginning.

The gleaming, spotlessly clean and grossly under-used plastic injection-moulding machine stood idle, gathering dust today. There wasn't even anybody to flick the dust off from time to time as, by agreement with Lady

Prosser, Joss had taken time out to think through his strategy for the company's recovery.

That, at least, was how Lady Prosser saw it. For his part however, Joss just needed some time to get his head together — the world was going too fast for him, and all he wanted to do was get off. He hadn't breathed a word of it to Fleur, partly because he wasn't sure just what it all meant, and partly because if she suspected promotion might be in the offing, he'd be under even greater pressure to do whatever it was he was supposed to do.

He'd left for work at the usual time that morning, so as not to arouse Fleur's curiosity. Sporting his clean, floral patterned, bell-bottomed overalls, flower power kipper tie and Cuban heeled boots, he'd headed for the factory until he was out of sight, then just kept on walking — for miles.

With the factory behind him he was trying to put his problems behind him too, just for long enough to clear his mind. He wouldn't know a business plan if it hit him in the face, and as for clitoral thinking — or whatever it was she'd asked him to do — he'd found it hard enough doing any kind of thinking. Not that he'd tried it all that often, but when he had it only led to trouble. Thinking was very much Fleur's department, she was good at it, but this time he was on his own — and it hurt.

By the time he reached Fairacre Farm he didn't have a clue where he was, all he knew was that his feet were aching even more than his brain. That at least was something new to think about and, for a few brief seconds, the words 'BUSINESS' and 'PLAN', which had continually flashed in his mind like some defective neon sign, were replaced by the thought of blisters beginning to form on his heels and the balls of his feet. He was also starting to get hungry.

Taking the footpath alongside the farmhouse and up onto the ridge overlooking Farthing Fflitch, he found the softer, more yielding, earth a little easier on his aching feet. He found apples and pears in the orchard close to the path, and pocketed a few choice specimens before scurrying off like a naughty schoolboy to enjoy his ill-gotten gains.

By now his mind was concentrating totally on not being found out. He must get off the beaten track before eating, so he headed for the concealment of a small copse where, by the side of a spring which fed the stream leading to the river, he took off his shoes and socks, cooled his feet in the crystal clear water, and started munching. Then back they came.

Those same two words haunted him, just hanging there in the vast void of his mind. It was as if, by concentrating hard on them, he might be able to fathom their meaning but, no matter how hard he tried, nothing flowed. He tried changing the positions of the words — after all there aren't too many options with a two word phrase — but that got him nowhere. He even tried jumbling the letters into an anagram, but 'LENA'S PISS BUN' took him ages to assemble, and still didn't get him anywhere.

He was just on the point of giving up, having come to the conclusion he just wasn't cut out for all this head stuff, when a very strange thought occurred to him. It wasn't so much a thought as a colour, a tiny dot of it way in the back of his mind, but it persisted. Gradually it grew, larger and more intense, until his head was filled with the most brilliant, all-absorbing, strangely relaxing pigmentation.

It became the most important thing in his life, his very existence, nothing else mattered, except green. And through the green came a clearer perspective, a new dawn of understanding seemingly beckoning him towards its labyrinth of knowledge.

So just what is it that's troubling you, he heard himself think, what's causing you all this suffering? Come on now, slowly and carefully, let's have it. The meeting with Emilia began to emerge, every word, every intonation, even her benign smile, the thoughts behind those words starting to take shape as he steadily built up the whole picture.

And you're the one chosen to resolve these problems, right? Well now, let's carefully think through just what the business has going for it at the moment. A good, experienced, loyal work force — that's a positive start, what else? Gradually he was able to build up a picture of the firm's attributes then, piece by piece, he was able to examine the problems

Right, so there's been a bit of a scandal involving the top man, but does that in any way affect the performance of the products? Do the end users, the true consumers in other words, feel in any way tainted as a result of Prosser's stupidity? Of course not, they probably don't even know who makes the products, all they care about is the end result. It'll be necessary to rebuild confidence, of course, and that's going to take time but, for a business which has been around as long as this one, selling its track record over the longer term shouldn't prove impossible.

In the meanwhile, however, we're faced with a cashflow problem. We need to generate business of a different nature to tide us over, so let's take another look at those attributes. Ah yes, we have machinery capable of handling plastics. Can we perhaps make other plastic products for a while? Maybe a little modification will be necessary, but that can all be accurately costed into our equation.

There must be a million and one products made from plastic, what we need to do now is research the market, find a niche which isn't being fully satisfied, then identify how much consumers will pay for that product. It then becomes a number crunching exercise as we move into the fields of marketing and distribution, plotting the effect on total sales volume of different price levels against production costs at those sales levels. When the optimum output, price and sales forecast have been decided upon, together with the set-up costs, we will have the basis of a business plan.

Brilliant, he thought, why didn't I think of it before? The reason you didn't think of it before, he realised, is that you were on your own. Oh, yes, of course I was. Here, hang about, I'm on my own now aren't I? Well, no you're not, actually. We're with you now.

The green colour faded, giving way to the very deepest purple he'd ever experienced. Slowly it receded into what he thought were four almonds in a horizontal row, surrounded by the green which, in itself was now taking on a shape, dividing into two in the process.

Eventually Joss could make out faces — odd, wrinkled faces with round, stubby noses and thin lips surrounding almond-shaped mouths — attached by strong, thick necks to small, emaciated bodies. He could have sworn these shapes were not only real, but standing right in front of him, but dismissed it as a trick of the mind — it wouldn't have been the first time his mind had played tricks on him, usually under the influence of the Shafton Rose.

But the only vegetable material he'd ingested today came from those apples and pears, and they couldn't possible contain hallucinatory chemicals — could they? Well then how could he explain the sudden clarity of mind which helped him understand the business plan?

Joss was becoming intrigued, and not a little uneasy.

His unease was about to become a full scale panic as he realised he couldn't shift these weird, green apparitions from his mind — they just continued getting clearer and clearer. He could now distinguish leaves surrounding them as they stood in the bushes, far more afraid of this giant sitting in front of them than he was of them. He could see their hair — long, dull, green hair which hung around their faces, over their puny shoulders and down their backs.

Their heads seemed totally out of proportion to the size of their bodies, and large, bat-like ears protruded through the hair. Simultaneously, and very gently, they raised their small, open hands — as if to show they were not carrying weapons. He couldn't help noticing the six digits on each hand, four long bony fingers and a thumb at each end. And a definite smile spreading across the faces, from the toothless mouths right up to those brightly shining, deep purple eyes.

Please don't hurt us, Joss heard himself think, we mean you no harm. We are simply weary travellers in search of rest and food and, if we may be permitted, we would also like to buy a small piece of your precious metal, aluminium.

Now convinced they were real, and sure they wouldn't do him any harm — they were even smaller than his granny for goodness sake — he beckoned them closer and smiled.

"You not from round 'ere then whack?"

chapter 6

"An' 'ee can stick they two bars back in that cattle grid an' all, an' if they goes missin' again I shall run 'ee in my lad."

PC Runstable was laying down the Law, after all, you didn't get to be a bastion of Law and Order if you didn't lay down the Law every once in a while. Frankie Fflitch was on the receiving end this time, being told to keep his clan well and truly away from the cordoned-off area — once he'd replaced the bars.

Runstable was well aware that the Fflitches rarely, if ever, left the hamlet, so shutting off their lane for a few days wouldn't present any hardship — besides they could always use their bridge to gain access to the main Hampton Road if they really had to go out anywhere.

His road blocks were now being set up at the Hatch End junction and at the hamlet end of the lane, the young copper on each having strict instructions to allow nobody through without a pass. The five-barred gate by the cattle grid was to be the main access to the site, so the third officer, PC Nick Pennington, was positioned there.

Pennington, for his sins, was also Scout Master of the 2nd Hampton Magna Scout Troop and, using his initiative, had brought much of the Troop's gear with him on what appeared to be a potentially long job. The ridge tent was positioned just inside the gate, to provide shelter for the officer on sentry duty, and somewhere for the lucky devil scheduled off watch to get his head down for a few hours. Runstable was particularly pleased to see the latrines tent being erected, but none too happy at the prospect of the rest of the world seeing his ankles, with his trousers around them, as he squatted over the makeshift chemical bucket.

With all his officers now in position, and with the Law well and truly laid down with the Fflitches, task-force commander Runstable allowed himself a little self-satisfied smile at a job well done as he returned to his car, parked alongside the river in the tiny hamlet. His reverie was short lived, however, when he noticed a flat tyre on his front nearside wheel.

Off came his tunic, up went his sleeves, out came the wheel brace, jack and spare wheel and in he got stuck, much to his annoyance. Not that he wasn't well versed in the art of wheel changing, far from it, but task-force commanders shouldn't be expected to perform such menial jobs, they have far weightier problems to think about.

After slackening the wheel nuts and jacking up the car, he removed the nuts and placed them in the upturned hubcap for safe keeping — as laid down in Standing Orders; Wheels, Changing Of, in his Police manual. You didn't get to be a task-force commander without going by the book.

"Foxtrot thirteen from Sierra Foxtrot, come in Foxtrot thirteen" squawked his personal radio. Recognising the voice instantly as that of Inspector Hector, Runstable jumped up quickly, snapping off a very smart salute as he came to attention, stamping his right foot down sharply on the upturned hubcap. He watched with mouth agape as all four nuts catapulted into the air, over his shoulder, and into the murky depths of the raging river with a gentle splash.

"Foxtrot thirteen from Sierra Foxtrot, come in Foxtrot thirteen" repeated his radio, but Runstable stood rigidly to attention, still saluting and with his jaws locked open, as he contemplated his latest logistical problem.

"FOXTROT THIRTEEN!" screamed the radio, "WHERE THE HELL ARE YOU RUNSTABLE?"

"Er, 'ere sir, I mean, er, Sierra Foxtrot from Foxtrot thirteen, go 'head Sierra Foxtrot."

"About time too Runstable. Your visitors are on their way, should be with you in thirty, that's three zero, minutes, got that?"

"Right sir, we'll be ready sir."

"Good. See to it that you are, I don't want any slip-ups on this job. Sierra Foxtrot out."

What the hell was he going to do now? As the senior officer, nay, task-force commander, he ought to be there to greet his visitors, but without his wheel nuts he was going nowhere.

"Oy, over yer a minute, I needs your 'elp" he yelled, spotting the Land Rover returning from cattle grid refurbishment duties. Nip down 'ampton fer I will 'ee, I needs four wheel nuts fer this un yer, an 'urry up 'bout it."

"Can't be done boss" replied Frankie. "Can't take it over the bridge, 'tis too 'eavy like, an' can't go up the lane — 'ee told I not to."

"Ar, but that were then, an' this is now, an' now I be tellin' 'ee to go" insisted the frustrated plod, "an' 'ee gotta do what I says now, not what I said then."

"But 'ang on a minute" remonstrated Frankie, "When 'ee told I not to go, that were 'now' — when 'ee told I like. Bain't 'now' now though, it be 'then', even I knows that, but 'twere 'now' when 'ee told I not to go. An' 'ee juss said I gotta do what 'ee tells I now — so bugger off." With that he turned on his heels and was gone, leaving a very confused Runstable still trying to work it out.

Returning to the car, growing more anxious by the minute, he stood looking at the wheel and scratching his head, wishing he hadn't got out of bed this morning.

"'Tis easy 'nough to sort that un out, my dear" he heard, but from whence he hadn't a clue. It was a woman's voice, of that he was certain — you didn't get to be an accomplished crime fighter without knowing the difference between men's voices and women's voices — and quite elderly as well, he would say. But where the hell was she?

"All 'ee gotta do, my dear, is take one of they nutty things off the other three wheels, then 'ee'll 'ave three to go on that 'un 'ont 'ee?"

Bloody 'ell, why didn't I think of that, thought our crime fighting mastermind. Because it wasn't in the Police manual, that's why, he realised. Original thinking like that ought to be rewarded with promotion, maybe he'd send it up as a suggestion to the editor of 'The Job', as an example of what he was capable of under pressure. That would make top brass sit up and think.

"I were juss thinkin' that meself" he replied, "at least it'll get I to 'ampton if I drives slowly. Wer be 'ee too any road?"

"Up yer my darlin'" called Fenella from her perch in the willow tree on the river bank. It was one of her favourite spots to while away a few hours, watching the trout in the river below as she got slowly inebriated on methylated spirit.

"'Ee don't want to be drinkin' that stuff, 'tis bad fer 'ee" insisted our upholder of solid virtues. "Besides, can't 'ee find no work to do, 'stead of wastin' 'ee time like that?"

"Nar, they 'ont let I do nothin'. Says I be crazy they do, out me 'ead like. Bain't nothin' wrong with I though, 'tis they buggers who'm soft in the 'ead. Be a lot 'appier if I did 'ave summat to do mind, but they 'ont let I."

"Well 'ee just leave it with old Ron Runstable. I'll go 'ave a word with Frankie presently, tell 'im ther bain't nothin' wrong with 'ee — 'e'll listen to I 'e will."

He could tell by her toothless smile that she was grateful, and impressed by his authority — after all, you didn't get to be a respected member of the establishment without helping those less fortunate than yourself. A social outcast she may be, but his years of experience told him there was nothing wrong with her mental faculties — blimey there was senior officers with scrambled egg on their hats less intelligent than her.

As he returned to the car to put his new found plan into action he felt a thud on the back of his head. It must have been several minutes before he came round, only to find himself sprawled across the road with an empty meths bottle lying alongside him and, as he raised his aching head, he heard Fenella screeching — "Don't forget to tell Frankie, will 'ee!"

"Mornin' sir, may I see your pass please? Very good, all in order sir, please continue" smiled the young officer as he raised the barrier. The MOD boffin in the back of the car returned the smile, clearly impressed, but his older colleague remained impassive as ever.

"Mornin' sir, pass please" demanded Pennington as the car approached the five-barred gate. The boffin was less pleased this time, surely the two officers had radio contact, in which case this one should know who he was and be prepared for his arrival. Besides he'd only just put the damned thing back in his wallet.

"Pass, please sir" insisted Pennington before he'd open the gate, "I have my orders, sir."

Officious little turd, thought the boffin, digging out his wallet again. He was even less pleased as the gate was closed behind his car, the same procedure being demanded individually of all eight Land Rovers behind him. His boss remained inscrutable.

Sir Gordon Bacon was a curious man who, as an MOD Section Head, had a reputation for brilliance throughout the Ministry. He was on first name terms with the Minister of Defence, and even received personally signed Christmas cards from the Prime Minister — much to the annoyance of the mandarins to whom he reported.

After graduating from Oxford with a First Class Honours Degree in History he was keen to make a career in the Army, but was turned down on medical grounds. You might think that a little odd for someone who gained blues in rugby and rowing, but when it came to the Army's aptitude test he was all fingers and thumbs — and the Army doesn't have a stock of gloves with six digits on the left hand.

He was snapped up very quickly by the Ministry of Defence, however, where his brain was put to very good use in matters of tactical planning and logistics, but it was in the field of nuclear weapons, back in the sixties, that he first came to prominence, gaining his knighthood into the bargain.

By the mid seventies he was heavily involved in aerospace projects — including a spell on assignment to NASA in Houston, Texas, where he met and married his wife, Lulu-Belle, now Lady Lulu-Belle Bacon, twenty-two years his junior and heiress to an oil fortune.

That's about as much as is publicly known about Sir

Gordon, the periods prior to, and after, these events appear shrouded in secrecy. Only those in the higher echelons of the defence establishment, together with those in his section, are aware of the true nature of his work and its ramifications throughout the world — and beyond.

Suffice it to say, for the time being, that not a single reported UFO sighting misses his department's attention, as well as thousands which are not publicly reported — by the RAF and the national air forces of other countries throughout the world. His hand-picked team of specialists are the finest in their respective fields, by a long way, and they don't understand the meaning of cuts in the defence budget. They don't need to.

The boffin now leading the team investigating case SF13942/3 FARTHING FFLITCH couldn't help wondering just why his boss had shown so much interest in this one. There appeared to be nothing unusual about it, a couple of reported sightings — admittedly one by a Police officer, but that wasn't particularly odd, even if the officer in question was — and a few corn circles. Big deal.

By rights it should simply become part of the statistical report on Sir Gordon's desk at the end of the month, just another bread and butter case, but he'd latched onto this one the minute the initial report hit their computer screens. Was he just wanting to keep his hand in? Did he have nothing better to do? Or had his incredible instinct led him to this one, as it had with so many other major developments?

Whatever the reason, there was no room for error on this case. Everything would have to be checked, double-checked, and then gone over once again for good measure — Sir Gordon didn't suffer fools lightly, and mistakes were things made by lesser mortals.

Working quickly but with supreme purpose of mind, the scientific team went into action — each member to his alloted task. The field was positively bristling with electronics, requiring the combined power output of eight Land Rovers, all driving generators linked to a central voltage regulator to protect the delicate equipment.

There were aerials, dishes, reflectors and probes, electron microscopes, soil core samplers — and a weird looking contraption looking remarkably like a water bed.

It's function was known only to one member of the team, the boffin who assembled it, plus of course Sir Gordon. It was secreted away inside a large tent, well away from curious eyes. The rest of the team may be expected to sleep on camp beds — if they could spare the time — but Sir Gordon travelled first class.

Neither would he travel without essential rations, and these he did share with the team — at least in part. After all, there was only room on such an expedition to bring one chef, so his culinary expertise may as well be put to good use in keeping up morale. Sir Gordon would have nothing tinned, frozen or micro-waved, so the venison and fresh asparagus tips had to be brought down by Harrods, whilst the Fortnum & Mason delivery driver brought the Beluga caviare and oak-smoked salmon.

The wines travelled in the back of one of the Land Rovers, specially adapted with foam rubber wine racks to absorb the bumps. Sir Gordon could smell a bruised wine a mile off.

All these little pleasures of life he gladly shared with his staff, but the stock of old Armagnac brandies and crusted Wellington ports were his, and his alone. As was the cocaine.

This charming little habit — sticking a glass tube up

his nose and snorting sharp, crushed crystals into his nostrils until they bled — was introduced to him by Lady Bacon, it being a prerequisite to any good dinner party for the Houston glitterati circles in which she moved. The supply of such products, even of the finest uncut quality, is never a problem for one in his position, of course, thanks to that age-old and rather quaint custom afforded to Embassy staff worldwide — the untouchable diplomatic bag.

For lunch the chef was preparing a venison ragout, cooked in red wine with the delicate bouquet of fresh, fine herbs. For those downwind of the chuck wagon it afforded occasional relief from the dreadful Farthing Fflitch stench, but the others just had to grin and bear it, true professionals that they were.

It didn't take Ron Runstable long to cotton on to the new, and very welcome, aroma. He had a nose for these things, and you didn't get to be an ace detective without having a nose for these things.

He also had what felt like a nose on the back of his head, due to his earlier altercation with the meths bottle. He was right, mind you, meths can do a body a lot of damage — especially at that speed and from that altitude. The lump was, by now, throbbing away quite effectively and his vision was becoming exceedingly blurred, but there was no question of his going off duty, not while he was task-force commander.

"Any chance of a bit of that ther stew fer me an' the lads then" he politely enquired of the chef, "only we ain't 'ad no dinner yet, nor no breakfast come to think of it."

"Peess off" came the sardonic reply, "I cook for ze, 'ow you say, er, ze grinder of ze organ, not 'is monkay."

The words 'slimey' and 'frog' immediately sprang to the hungry task-force commander's mind, but he thought better of using them — it could cause a diplomatic incident. Men of power have to think of these things.

A quick check with Nick Pennington and the other lads revealed that they had come prepared, each with a pile of sandwiches and a flask of tea, now duly consumed, and so he was the only one with a rumbling stomach. And an aching head. And yet another logistical problem.

He couldn't leave the site, that would never do, so he would somehow have to contact Ruby and have his dinner brought round to him. There were no phones on site, nor in the hamlet, and he couldn't use his Police radio to order grub, he'd be up on a charge quick as a flash. Then he had a brainwave, a rare event indeed, but one of which he was quite proud — maybe he was senior officer material after all.

"Sierra Foxtrot from Foxtrot thirteen, come in Sierra foxtrot"

"Sierra Foxtrot, go ahead Ron."

"Ah, Sarge, urgent message for me missis, 'ould 'ee be good 'nough to phone 'er please?"

"Better be good, Ron, you know the rules on personal calls."

"'Tis genuine Police business, Sarge, I needs to know if they buggers in Shafton is plannin' to try an' get into this site 'cross the fields. I got a informer in the village, 'er'd know if they was."

"What's your snout's name?"

"Patsy, tell 'er I gotta get 'old of Patsy, urgent."

"OK, Ron, leave it with me. Sierra Foxtrot out."

Pleased with his little deception, Runstable took a stroll around the site, feeling very important. There was no informant of course, Patsy was Ruby's name for those delicious Cornish Pasties made by Vera Hardcastle, of the VerKen bed and breakfast in Weston-Super-Mare.

Each year, on their annual pilgrimage to that veritable mecca of good living, Ron and Ruby would take them freshly caught trout from the river Test and, in return, they would bring back a couple of boxes of freshly made Cornish Pasties for the freezer.

Ruby would know, instantly, what his message meant, dig one out and stick it in the microwave. Should take about fifteen minutes to defrost, a couple of minutes to heat up, and ten minutes to drive here with it. No more than half an hour at the outside, he only hoped she'd realise he'd need a cup of tea with it — he never had a pasty without a cup of tea.

"Do 'ee wanna know anythin' else 'bout that ther spaceship then, sir" he enquired of the boffin idly, whilst awaiting his pasty, "only I could point 'ee in the right direction like, show 'ee wer it come from an' all."

"No thank you, constable, that won't be necessary."

"Well per'aps I could take one of they instruments of yorn an' go see if I can't find the bugger. I knows which way 'e wer 'eadin' like."

"That's very kind of you, constable, but perhaps you'd better leave this to us. Thank you."

"Bain't no trouble, sir, I don't mind goin' lookin' for it. Just give I one of they bits of gear, this 'un yer looks 'andy . . ."

"Constable, that Irradiation Frequency Modulator you've just picked up has cost the taxpayer one hundred and thirty five thousand pounds. It is extremely delicate and, once it is set, the slightest vibration can cause irreparable damage. Now if you do not put it down at once, very gently, I shall have your gonads removed with an extremely blunt instrument and have them pinned to your helmet for a souvenir. Am I making myself clear?"

Runstable made his excuses and left hurriedly. A

task-force commander has a hundred and one things to oversee, has to keep his finger on the pulse like, besides his dinner shouldn't be long now.

"'Ello, 'ello, Ruby, what you doin' 'ere?" asked the young officer at the barrier.

"Got summat fer me 'usband, 'aven't I, all right if I goes through?"

"Sorry Ruby, can't let anybody through without a pass, Ron would 'ave me guts for garters."

Pasties were off today.

chapter 7

There are any number of fine specimens caught in Hampshire's famous trout streams and rivers each year, but the whopper spotted by Fenella from her perch in the willow tree would have given any angler an orgasm. It must have been 14 lbs if it was an ounce and that, for a brown trout, is a very serious fish.

She could hardly contain herself as she slid down the tree, skinning her shins in the process. That mattered not a hoot, what did matter was that there was a big fish about — one that would bring paying anglers down to Farthing Fflitch — and she had been the first to spot it.

"Frankie, oy, Frankie" she yelled, running barefoot through the hamlet as if her very life depended on it, "come see what I seen".

Frankie was whittling away at a piece of wood, one of his favourite pastimes as he sat in the late afternoon sunshine. The shape he was carving had started, like they all did, as a huge trout which he would sell to anglers who had no other trophies to take home but, like all the others, it was doomed to end up as yet another clothes peg.

Resolving to do something about the huge pile of wood shavings outside his hovel one of these days — unless good fortune in the shape of a hurricane beat him to it — he glanced across at Fenella as she zig-zagged down the lane at breakneck speed, taking care not to spill any of her precious methylated spirit.

"Come quick . . . come . . . quick," urged the breathless crone, "'tis a . . . soddin' girt . . . brownie, . . . biggest I . . . ever seen."

"Oh ar, an' 'ow big be 'e then" replied her cousin, considerably more interested in the blasted knot of hard wood, right where the dorsal fin should be. It would take hours to carve the delicate, spiny, shape in that lot, then the sodding knot would probably fall out anyway — and who'd want to buy a wooden trout with a spare arsehole halfway down its back? It might make a good clothes peg though.

"I tell 'ee Frankie" she continued, slowly regaining her breath if not her composure as she swallowed another huge slug from the bottle — how she could eat those slimey, disgusting, creatures was beyond Frankie, but each to her own — "it be as long as a bit of string."

"An' 'ow long be a bit of string then?" he enquired philosophically, taking an axe to his masterpiece. It would make two nice clothes pegs now.

She tried hard to remember just which piece of string, amongst all the rubbish on the river bank, she'd used as her yardstick. Was it the one with several knots in it which lay amongst the decomposing tea bags, or was it perhaps the grubby bit of old sisal which snaked around the perished bicycle tyre? She was becoming confused.

Forgetting about the string she concentrated on the fish again and remembered that, when she first caught sight of it from her perch twenty feet above the river, she'd been in mid-swig. She'd gazed in sheer bewilderment at this magnificent creature, quite unable to remove the bottle from between her gums, as it fought the current below her.

She particularly remembered seeing its head to the left of her bottle whilst the tail flicked furiously beyond the other side — so it must be bigger than the width of her bottle. Standing before her increasingly disinterested cousin now, holding the bottle at arm's length, it didn't seem terribly big at all.

Maybe she was imagining things, it had, after all, been a two bottle day — what with all the comings and goings, and that copper raising her hopes and all. Fenella was settling quite nicely into one of her depressed moods as she slumped to the ground alongside Frankie, who was wondering if he could in fact get three pegs out of it now.

"Unkie Frankie, Unkie Frankie" screamed Fanny as she tore down the lane in their direction, "come quick, come quick — big fish in water Unkie Frankie, come and see, now."

It was indeed rare for his niece to get so excited, but he really didn't take too kindly to a grown woman, fully ten years his senior, calling him Unkie Frankie, even if her father was his older brother. But his mother was Fanny's mother's niece, so by rights she was his great aunt Fanny. Such are the ways of Farthing Fflitch.

But two reports of big fish in as many minutes were enough to set the adrenalin coursing through his veins and that familiar, comfortable, itch to break out across his left palm. His fingers cupped themselves automatically as he contemplated the angling fees, not to mention the cattle-grid gratuities — once those interfering coppers had finished snooping around the corn field.

Way up on the ridge, Joss was getting to know his newfound friends — now that he'd got used to them speaking to him from inside his own head. They were totally unlike anybody else he'd ever met, not just in physical appearance — although that had, admittedly, taken a bit of getting used to — but in the way communication just flowed.

He was usually very awkward with people he didn't know, and absolutely hated all the polite badinage of opening conversations. "And where do you come from, Joss?", "So what do you do to earn a crust, Joss" and all the other, probing, opening gambits were anathema to a bloke who didn't want to be probed, but he had to go through it — mainly for Fleur's sake, she was the gregarious type, but not Joss, he was perfectly happy in his comfortable little world.

Yttrium and Argona had no need of such small talk, they already knew more about Joss than he knew himself. Scanning the memory of an Einstein would be a simple task, once they'd got their prospect into intellectual focus, but they'd been surprised just how little they'd gleaned from Joss. It was as if they'd been searching a vast, empty, cave for treasure and found little for their trouble but a few rusty baked bean cans. Maybe he was trying to hide something from them. Time would tell.

Oddly enough, Joss found that it was he who was doing all the probing, his quest for knowledge becoming insatiable all of a sudden. Where did they come from? How did they get here? Had the journey been bad? Was the traffic terrible? Had they eaten yet? He offered to take them home to meet Fleur, and maybe stay for a bite to eat. Fleur was doing liver and bacon tonight, they'd like that.

By 'liver' do you mean what I think you mean, thought Yttrium, an internal organ from another being? Another biped perhaps? Do you really eat each other? These beings were even more barbaric than he'd realised.

"No you daft sod" laughed Joss out loud, "we don't

eat people, not unless we wanna get locked up like, it's only pig's liver — we don't eat our own kind you know." Argona was relieved to learn that, but far from happy about the thought of eating another living being — and even less enamoured at the thought that she, too, might be considered edible by the bipeds.

Graciously declining the offer, for the time being at least, Yttrium cast a curious glance at the apples Joss had brought with him. He knew the bipeds ate them as he'd seen Joss stuffing his fat little face with them, and he couldn't help wondering what they tasted like.

He smiled graciously as one was handed gently to him, and carefully held it to his mouth. He sucked cautiously at first, then with great vigour and, within a matter of seconds, all that remained was a pure white apple. Not a molecule of moisture or pigmentation remained, just a perfectly white, apple-shaped object which simply disintegrated into a tiny pile of dust.

Joss couldn't believe what he'd just witnessed as he handed a pear to Argona, only to watch it disappear the same way, the dust dissolving into the undergrowth about their feet as her eyes probed for more fruit. Gladly he gave up the remainder of his ill-gotten gains, and promised to show his new whackers where they could help themselves to more when they were ready.

Argona spotted a flurry of activity in the hamlet below them, and stealthily made her way to the edge of the copse to get a better view, leaving Yttrium and Joss to their own devices. Winding down his telepathic output to a weak, unidirectional beam in Joss' direction, Yttrium confided the fact that it was Argona's birthday tomorrow, and was there any chance of a little help in finding a piece of aluminium. Nothing too large or ornate, she wasn't a greedy girl, just a little souvenir of their visit.

No problem whack, thought Joss, leave it with me — now just run that business plan stuff through me one more time, just to be certain like, he urged as the pair set off to find out what was holding Argona's attention.

There below them the corn field was awash with odd-looking pieces of equipment, some flashing, others humming as their weird antennae swept the skies, but it was the activity in the hamlet itself which gave the greatest cause for concern, as people ran excitedly towards the spot where the vehicle was parked.

"Down 'ere Unkie Frankie, down 'ere — look. Told 'ee didn' I Unkie Frankie?" Fanny was pointing excitedly to a small shoal of very large brown trout, each the equal of Fenella's monster, as they grubbed around on the bottom in their search for food, just downstream of the vehicle.

The excitement had brought out dozens more cousins, and Frankie was now trying desperately to calm them before their stampede frightened the little beauties away. All he had to do now was catch one, take it to the landlord at 'The One That Got Away', just up the river, and the angling press would be onto it in a flash — bringing the Tweed-jacketed, thigh-booted, multi-rodded big spenders rolling in to Farthing Fflitch within days.

Messing about with a fancy piece of feather tied to a hook wasn't Frankie's way, that was strictly for the ponces who wanted to spend all day showing others how they could make it look like a fly, getting it to dance on the water until the mesmerised trout rose to the bait.

Neither was dynamiting to be recommended in the circumstances, given that the local constabulary were well within earshot — besides he wanted to leave a few in there for the anglers to catch, then even more anglers would be lining up to pay their fees. No, perhaps the old ways were best for this particular job.

Rolling up his sleeve he took up his position, lying flat on his stomach at the very edge of the river bank with his legs wide apart, and gently slid his left hand into the water, almost up to his armpit. There he waited patiently, his hand and arm becoming numb with cold, until curiosity got the better of one of the trout.

Was that a nice, tasty, bunch of six worms swaying to and fro in the water? The inquisitive fish just had to find out — not too quickly though, you never know what dangers lurk amongst these waters, even hunger has to wait until a chap is certain. There are old fish and there are bold fish, but there are no old, bold fish in this stretch of river.

Slow and sure, that's the motto if you want to become a big fish around here — unless of course you've been feeding around that new boulder. Quite remarkable piece of feeding ground that, he must have put on pounds recently, but those gently wriggling worms near the bank did look rather tasty, and they weren't going to stay there for ever now, were they? If he didn't have them someone else would, and damned quickly too, so maybe they were worth a closer peek.

Very gingerly he approached the target area from downstream, using the force of the river to balance his carefully controlled swimming strength as he inched closer and closer. It was indeed a very strange odour coming from these worms, in fact he wasn't at all sure they were worms now, but what the devil were they?

It was a puzzling question, and one any self-respecting fish has to find an answer to, but perhaps from a safer distance. As he turned to move away, one of the fingers stroked his underside, an experience he found quite arousing — almost reminiscent of courting time. A chap could quite get to like this.

A few more, gentle, strokes left him feeling really rather good and, as more fingers joined in the well-orchestrated serenade on his senses, memories of last season's erotic pleasures came flooding back, how that delightful young filly had teased him with her provocative dancing, the sheer ecstasy of it — even now it caused his entire body to tremble at the thought of it.

Once a chap's gone rigid with desire he's putty in anybody's hands, and Frankie's were about as skilful as they come. In an instant the scooping left hand had its quarry flying through the air, landing several feet back on the bank as the cousins whooped and clapped around the gasping, flapping fish.

"That were my bugger, I seen 'im first" sobbed Fenella, who'd hauled herself up from her oblivion to join in the action, only to find her cousins congratulating Fanny on being the first to spot it, "I told Frankie 'bout 'im, didn' I Frankie?"

But Frankie was far too busy to get involved in family arguments, he had other fish to fry.

Not sure whether to stuff it with almonds and fry it in butter, or stuff it with cotton wool and mount it in glass, the landlord of 'The One That Got Away' drooled over Frankie's catch with sheer envy — and the knowledge that there were more, just ready for the taking, certainly fired the enthusiasm of his angling journalist pals in London.

Leaving a warm, comfortable bed — complete with equally warm, comfortable wife — in the middle of the night to go haring off into the countryside, there to spend every possible daylight hour up to one's backside in cold water, may not be every man's idea of a wet dream. But these boys were well and truly hooked.

Their four-wheel drive cars were kept fully laden, with thousands of pounds worth of rods, landing nets, keep nets, line of every conceivable gauge and breaking strain, hooks of every size and a collection of artificial flies which would astound any true entomologist.

Lap top computers enabled them to write up their copy at the river bank and mobile fax machines, coupled to their car phones, would enable them to get it to the editor's desk within minutes. Their's was a serious business, the highly popular sport of angling attracting more fans than soccer — and these fans could read.

"Mornin' sir, pass please" greeted the first of the journalists to arrive at the Hatch End road block. This just had to be some kind of a wind-up of course, one of his competitors had got here before him and left this stripagram character to delay him, if not put him off altogether. Some chance.

"Very funny Mr Plod, now if you'll excuse me some of us have serious work to do" laughed the bleary-eyed journalist, knocking over the traffic cones as he sped down the lane. How on earth the agency had the neck to send out a 'Policeman' looking like that he'd never know, he was far too young. He was determined to find out which of his competitors had tried to stitch him up though, he'd have the bastard.

At the five barred gate a desperately hungry and very tired task-force commander had relieved the young Nick Pennington, who was now snoring soundly inside his tent. There was absolutely no human activity going on in the field behind him, other than sleeping, as all the data-collecting instruments had been put into stand-by mode. Should anything occur they would spring into action, starting up the Land Rover engines automatically to provide full power, thus waking the crew.

But there'd not been so much as a peep all night, just the awful stench and the rumbling of his belly to keep Runstable awake. He was seriously regretting having submitted that blasted report, and was beginning to have doubts about what he'd seen with his own eyes when his radio broke the silence of the night.

"Foxtrot Thirteen from Thirteen Alpha, come in Foxtrot Thirteen" it squawked, shaking him out of his skin.

"Go 'head, Alpha" he whispered, not wishing to set those damned instruments off.

"Bloke's just broke through the road block, 'eadin' your way, can you deal?"

"Leave it with I, Foxtrot Thirteen out." "Course 'e's 'eadin' this way if 'e's broke through the bleedin' road block" Runstable muttered to himself as he woke his young colleague "an' course I can deal, 'tis what I be 'ere for bain't?"

But if somebody driving a car was intent on getting into the field, stopping them was not going to be easy — even with Pennington's help. And the old five barred gate had seen better days, any impact over three miles an hour would reduce it to firewood. Quick as a flash he raced out into the lane, where he could clearly hear the car racing towards him, grabbed the two loose bars from the cattle grid, and nipped back inside the gate.

There he and Pennington hammered them diagonally into the crumbling gateposts to bolster their defences. The noise triggered the sensitive equipment behind them, starting all the engines and bringing excited scientists rushing from their tents in various states of undress, just as the four wheel drive Suzuki locked up, skidding into the cattle grid, truly gridlocked.

As the incredulous hack stepped out of his car — first the fake Plod and now this, just what the hell was going on? — he heard the Land Rover engines racing away, saw all the flashing lights, could hear people yelling excitedly behind the hedgerow, and genuinely believed he'd stumbled across a moto-cross meeting — but in the middle of the night?

"What be 'ee doin' 'ere" yelled Runstable above the din, more angry at having torn his breeches climbing over the gate than anything else. He'd had to climb over, the bars had now jammed it completely — yet another logistical problem to add to his list.

"Just going fishing, officer" replied the hack, "but more to the point, what are you doing here — and what's going on in there?"

"That be for us to know, my lad" came the stern response as Runstable reached for his pocket book, "I'll be 'avin' 'ee name, if 'ee please. Going fishing indeed! At four o'clock of a soddin' mornin'?"

"No Law against that is there? It's what I happen to do for a living actually, and you have no right to apprehend me, nor indeed to require me to furnish you with any information, unless of course you suspect me of having committed a crime. This is still, is it not, a free country?"

"I see, clever bugger eh? Right then Mr Smartarse, 'ow 'bout, just for starters like, 'Failin' To Stop When So Required By A Police Officer In The Execution Of 'is Duty', then ther's 'Wilful Damage To Police Property, viz, two traffic cones', 'Drivin' Without Due Care And Attention', else 'ee 'ouldn't 'ave ended up in that lot 'ould 'ee, an' do 'ee want for I to add 'Failin' to Provide Identity When Lawfully So Required'? 'Tis up to 'ee like."

"Here's my Licence and Insurance, officer, any other information you'd like? Colour of hair? Sexual preferences? Inside leg measurement?"

"OK clever clogs, just 'ee stand over 'ere so's I can keep an eye on 'ee, while I gets this lot down" he ordered, marching the troublesome hack over to the gate, from where he could read the details more clearly under the arc light.

"Bloody Hell!" exclaimed the journalist at the sight of all the equipment. Neither had he missed the outline of the crop circles. There'd be copy on his editor's desk before daylight, and he'd not be unduly worried about the omission of any reference to fish, the International News Agencies would pay handsomely for this story.

chapter 8

"So what I gotta do, babe, is get all this stuff out me 'ead, like, an' onto paper. What d'ya think?"

Joss had plucked up enough courage to face his mentor, not only about his meeting with Emilia, but also about his new-found friends from Strontium — about whom he hadn't stopped enthusing all evening and even now, in the cold light of day, over breakfast.

At first Fleur had just put it down to a particularly bad trip, he had them occasionally when he got a little too high — especially if he had a few worries, like losing yet another job — but the delusion rarely lasted very long. This time, however, it seemed to have taken hold.

Everywhere she went in the village she was constantly assailed with yet another version of Ned's comeuppance at the pub, and wasn't it sad that he should end up like this — and now her husband was heading the same way. She resolved to drop by and have a chat with Doctor Foster as soon as possible, but in the meanwhile it was probably best just to humour him.

"Sure, hun, sounds cool to me and, if 'Emilia' goes for it, then who knows — could be our ticket to the big time. We've got all weekend, so why don't we start on it right now?"

"Magic, but before we do, like, I gotta take this bit of

aluminium to Yttrium. I promised 'im 'cause it's Argona's birthday an' it's 'er present, like."

"A bit of aluminium. Hmm, OK, any particular bit in mind?"

"Well 'e says 'e don't want nothing too big or fancy, just summat small an' light. Mebbiz we could take 'em a bit of tinfoil out the kitchen, like."

We? He did say "We" didn't he. Fleur had a thousand and one things to do today, and Mrs Merryweather was dropping by to collect her new twin set this afternoon. The lining wasn't even in it yet and the button holes had still to be sewn and cut, and she was being invited to go to goodness knows where, looking for little green people who collect tinfoil!

Still, at least he wouldn't come to any harm if she were with him and, when these space fairies failed to materialise, they might get back in time to enable her to finish Mrs Merryweather's outfit. There was also the possibility that a little fresh air and exercise might do him some good, enable him to get his head together. She wasn't holding her breath though.

"Got any veggies an' all, babe? Only they don't eat meat, like."

Loading up her plastic carrier bag with a brace each of carrots, onions, tomatoes and potatoes, together with a few runner beans from Ned's garden and a neatly folded piece of tinfoil, a single teardrop managed to escape her determined self control — a strength which had seen them through far worse scrapes than this — and joined the vegetables nestling in the bag.

"Yeah, course I will mate, no problem, see 'ee tonight." Georgie Smith couldn't believe his luck, a booking for three rooms on full bed, breakfast and evening meal terms — and no discount — and the bloke even gave him his credit card number over the phone so he could take full payment in advance — provided he kept the rooms, irrespective of what time they turned up, and didn't let them to anyone else.

There was just one tiny snagette — he only had two rooms to let, and they hadn't been used in ages. He planned to shift the stock of crisps, nuts and nibbles out of the box room and borrow a bed from somewhere — goodness knows where at such short notice — but the room would need a quick coat of white paint. Jill was going to be a busy girl today.

Jill was indeed very handy with a paintbrush, and had been long before she married Georgie, although canvas was her more accustomed medium rather than flaking plaster and peeling doorframes. However Georgie had got himself into yet another hole and, yet again, she would come to his rescue, goodness only knows why.

But with Georgie out looking for a bed and opening time looming ever closer, Jill was in a quandary. You can't just find bar staff at five minutes notice, and if she didn't open dead on time there'd be hell to pay so, dealing with her most urgent problem first, she put down her paint brush and opened up the bar.

She'd been serving non-stop for a good half an hour — and still no sign of Georgie — when she suddenly remembered her paintbrush. It would be going hard by now and, if she didn't do something about it quickly, it would be totally ruined.

She still couldn't get away from the bar so she asked Paddy to nip up to the box room, fill the paint kettle with white spirit, and work the brush around in it for a minute or two, that would save the day and enable her to clean it out properly later.

Damned expensive way of cleaning an old paint-brush, thought Paddy to himself, but who was he to question the lady of the house? So of he trotted, grabbing a couple of bottles of gin from the stockroom behind the bar on his way, and duly completed the task in hand — taking a few decent swigs from each bottle before pouring them into the paint kettle.

Now Georgie's sense of humour may be renown, and his taste for the absurd almost eccentric, but the funny side of this little episode eluded him somewhat. To say that he was not a happy chappy would be a masterpiece of understatement, and the unfortunate journalist who phoned that afternoon — to see if he had a room to let — got the full force of Georgie's vented spleen, especially when he offered to pay over the odds.

The realisation that he could have charged considerably more for his rooms was like rubbing salt into a gangrenous wound — but why the hell was there so much interest in Shafton all of a sudden? The question continued to plague him as he chalked up that evening's 'Special' on the blackboard behind the bar: 'WHITE DEMON' GIN COCKTAIL, £1 A GLASS.

All thoughts of Mrs Merryweather's twin set had completely deserted Fleur. Joss had been raving all night and all morning about little green people and now here they were — in the flesh, so to speak. And they were talking to her from inside her own head, so was Joss, an eerie experience which took a little getting used to.

But get used to it she did, and very quickly. She couldn't stop asking questions about Strontium, and was completely enthralled by their description of the long techni-coloured winters — so much so that Joss couldn't get a thought in sideways. They'd been rabbitting so long she almost forgot to give them the vegetables she'd hauled all the way up to the ridge.

The carrots were an immense hit, as were the tomatoes and runner beans — all disappearing into that white, almost translucent powder Joss had described. The potatoes were somewhat less impressive, although Argona had been very polite, they just lacked any kind of distinctive taste. The onions, on the other hand, were positively repulsive, causing the pair to shed a tear or two when the acid molecules reached their eyes.

The tiny yellow teardrops reminded Fleur about the tinfoil which lay, still neatly folded, in the bottom of her bag. Surely Joss had been mistaken about this, they couldn't possibly want this rubbish, could they? But when she saw the veritable flood of yellow tears streaming down Argona's face on receiving this gift, she felt as though she'd just handed over the Crown Jewels.

Very tenderly the long, bony, fingers unfolded the tinfoil, gently smoothing out the creases and, holding the shinier side towards her, she gazed at her reflection for ages. She'd not been able to do this for twelve years, it being considered unsafe to carry hard objects like mirrors on board the vehicle in case of turbulence, and the opportunity to take a long, hard, look at herself was too good to miss.

Of course, she'd been able to see herself through Yttrium's eyes whenever she wanted to, simply by scanning his mind whilst he focussed on her, but it wasn't the same. Men just don't see women the same way as women see themselves. Fleur understood perfectly.

"So what brings you boys down these 'ere parts then?" enquired Georgie, helping the journalists unload their car, "Bain't often we gets in the news, so to speak."

It hadn't been all that long since the place was simply heaving with hacks, all seeking an angle on the Prosser Drugs Scandal story from anybody who was prepared to open their mouth. Some of the comments attributed to the folks of the village were quite astounding, and even now you rarely heard the Widow Crabtree use words like "Egregious" or "Unmitigated", and Jack Marley wouldn't recognise "Unconscionable" if it smacked him in the face.

But such matters were of little consequence now, the name of the game now was to find out what the hell was going on, and how that knowledge could be used to good advantage.

"Good story, be it then, what you lads be on like?" he continued to probe, carrying the cases up the stairs with the journalists in his wake, "Only I might be able to point 'ee in the right direction, like, 'cause I knows one or two folks roun' yer. Anything I can 'elp 'ee with, like?"

"Don't think so pal" grunted Bill Morgan, clearly the senior member of the team from his very manner, and still tired and emotional from their previous refreshment break at a watering-hole the other side of Hampton, "not unless you know anything about flying saucers."

"Seen a few of they in me time, I can tell 'ee. Bain't safe to be in our kitchen when Jill be angry 'bout summat — cups, saucers, the lot goes flyin'" laughed Georgie, trying to jolly the conversation along.

"Just as I thought" remarked Morgan to his colleagues, rolling his eyes. He pummelled the mattress in the newly painted box room with his fist before deciding to allocate this room to the younger of his colleagues.

"Bain't nothin' to do with ol' Ned Thrubwell, be it?" suggested Georgie, trying to get the conversation back on track.

"And who, pray, is this Mr Thrubwell to whom you refer?" came the disinterested response as Morgan inspected the state of the next room. This one would probably suffice as his billet, but he'd keep his options open until the final room had been given the once-over.

"Ol' Ned? Bloody good mate of mine 'e be. Reckons 'e seen this 'ere spaceship down Farthin' Fflitch, dafty ol' bugger. Bain't what this be 'bout, be it?"

"Drinks here, does he?" replied Morgan, suddenly taking more interest in what Georgie had to impart. "Is he in tonight?"

"Oh ar, good little reg'lar be our Ned. Aint seen 'e yet though, want I to look out fer 'e do 'ee?" suggested Georgie, absent-mindedly allowing his palm to open. Morgan peeled a crisp £10 note from the roll in his pocket to seal the transaction, clearly he would very much like a word with Mr Thrubwell.

Leaving his guests to settle in Georgie returned to the bar, trying to figure out how best to get Ned into the pub. Should he just phone him and tell him to get his arse in gear? Maybe not, he was probably still smarting from his last visit. Should he send a message, telling him there was free beer waiting for him? But then he'd probably suspect he was being set up again. Well, perhaps he shouldn't get him in at all — not just yet — after all that was a decent sized roll in Morgan's pocket, and he seemed ready enough to part with it, maybe the passage of time coupled with a little more alcohol would ease the parting even more.

Up on the ridge the passage of time seemed but a twinkling of the eye. In their new-found friends, Joss and Fleur had discovered true soul mates, people who understood them perfectly and liked them for what they were. Pretence was unnecessary — indeed, totally pointless — as these two could see through it in an instant, like looking through glass, besides, they had nothing to hide.

For their part, Yttrium and Argona felt secure with these two bipeds. There was no malice in them and, even if they did eat other living beings, Strontians were clearly not on the menu. That may not necessarily be the case with other bipeds, nor indeed with other creatures who may inhabit this blue planet, which they now knew to be called Earth by the natives, so they would have to remain ever vigilant.

They found it strange that there should be different classes of bipeds. The primitive specimens, those who lived close to where the vehicle was parked, seemed to live such different lives to those now probing around the initial landing site — indeed they were physically separated from them by yet another class of being.

This was totally at odds with life on Strontium, there being only one distinction — you were either male or female. It was true that segregation of the sexes during their early, formative years, when education was of paramount importance, led to class distinction in later years.

It was also true that this, in turn, had led to a lack of equality of the sexes in years gone by but, little by little, the role of males in Strontian society had improved considerably to the point where they, at least, considered themselves equal to their counterparts.

Joss and Fleur seemed to be from a different class again to those down in the valley. They behaved differently, they spoke differently, and they certainly dressed differently, maybe they were from a separate tribe altogether.

"Maybe we are, man, maybe we are are", mused Fleur. "The peace tribe. And we have this, kind of like, tribal thing we share with our friends" she continued, reaching into her kaftan pocket for her leather pouch.

Those purple eyes never left her for a second, enthralled by the quaint little ceremony now unfolding in front of them as she built a joint. They almost jumped out of their skins, however, when she flicked her lighter, creating a flame. Fire wasn't something they were familiar with, there wasn't even a thought for it in their vocabulary, but it certainly fascinated them — almost beyond belief.

The fire was transferred to the joint and then extinguished, the cute little machine which created it having been put safely away. They watched as Fleur inhaled the smoke deeply, and felt the resulting surge of relaxation she experienced as the cares of her world melted away for a while.

She passed the joint to Argona and watched as those deep purple eyes concentrated on the strange, cylindrical, smouldering object she held between her inner thumb and forefinger, but hesitated not a second before copying the ritual Fleur had just performed. She coughed a little as the smoke entered her lungs, but was surprised how quickly she became accustomed to it.

Come on whack, Joss urged Yttrium, eager to watch him experience it too, but equally keen to have his own turn at the communal magic stick. By the time it had gone full circle, all four were sharing the same wonderful distortion of reality, the philosophical confluence profoundly examining the meaning of reality itself as they watched the big red star setting before them.

It's gonna be dark soon, like, thought Joss. Why don't the pair of youse come an' bed down in our pad, like? It'll be a lot safer than up 'ere, besides, we got loads more of them tomatoes an' stuff, an' it's kinda cosy.

With the sun's final quadrant slowly sinking behind the distant hills, the four linked hands and headed down the ridge towards Shafton. As the long shadows of the small thatched cottages crept out into the darkness behind them, the creatures of the night began to stir.

A small moth was the first to catch their collective attention, busily fluttering about in the gentle breeze, spilling minute dust particles from its wings as it flew in search of a mate.

Argona was the first to hear the sonar of the approaching bat, but it was only a fraction of a second before they were all tuned in to the same frequency, the clicks becoming louder and quicker as it moved in for the kill. The moth heard them too, but only just in time.

As the long, grasping claws extended from the furry body with its hideous, grinning face, the moth simply dropped out of the sky, leaving the bat grabbing nothing but air. Seemingly undeterred, the reckless moth continued on its travels, a journey which was destined to end very shortly and very painfully as the bat swooped in for another, and this time more successful, attack.

As the astounded foursome looked on, the bat plucked its meal from the sky and headed for home, leaving nothing behind but a small cloud of dust from the moth's wings. This is not a safe place to be, thought Yttrium, increasing the length of his stride as he urged the others onward.

When they reached the edge of the village it was Fleur who had a sudden attack of panic as reality returned to her senses. Once they came within the glare of the street lights they risked being seen, and their new friends were hardly inconspicuous. Joss' van was still being repaired at the garage, so he couldn't come and collect them in it. They'd somehow have to hide them, but how?

Still in the shadows, Joss slipped out of his kaftan, invited his friends to put their long, emaciated arms around his neck, then got Fleur to replace the coat. He was amazed at how light they were, hardly any weight at all as they hung down his sides like a pair of newspaper delivery bags, swinging backwards and forwards under the coat.

"Evenin' Mr and Mrs Stick" nearly gave all four of them a simultaneous heart attack.

"Oh, hi Mrs Crabtree, lovely evening isn't it. Just stepping out for a bit of fresh air and exercise" she proffered nervously as the elderly widow emptied the contents of her vacuum cleaner bag into her dustbin.

"Looks like 'e needs it an' all" she laughed, "puttin' on a bit of weight ain't 'e. 'Tis good 'ome cookin' what does that 'ee knows, my 'usband were just the same, God rest 'is soul."

The subtle warning well and truly heeded, they bade the widow a good night and continued their journey, hoping against hope it would be the last such chance meeting that night. But what if they were to bump into PC Runstable? That experienced old nose of his would know there was something afoot.

They quickened their pace a little more until they were almost jogging, Joss' passengers swinging wildly around his neck so that he resembled a sack full of monkeys having a pillow fight until, at last, the welcoming sight of their little cottage hove into a view.

Joss heaved a huge sigh of relief as he slipped his key into the lock. Safe at last.

"Evenin' whacker me ol' mate, any chance of a spot of that beer of yorn?"

Georgie was all smiles as his guests made their way to the bar for their pre-dinner drinks. He was well aware of the hard drinking reputation this particular profession had earned, and looked forward to a very busy evening.

"Evening Landlord" greeted Morgan, almost politely, "any sign of this Thrubwell fellow yet?"

"Er, not yet sir, might come in later though, I'll be sure to tell 'ee when 'e do. Now what can I get 'ee to drink then?"

"Gin and Tonics I think, that OK with you chaps?" he enquired of his keenly nodding, if somewhat subservient, colleagues. "Oh, hold up a minute, change of plan, I think we'll try your special. Yes, three White Demons please — and make them large ones."

chapter 9

Joss had found it very hard to ignore Ned on the doorstep, indeed he was torn between his loyalty to his old friend and his new ones.

It was left to Fleur to explain he didn't mean to appear rude, but that he was simply breaking his neck for a pee — an excuse Joss would have been well advised to remember when he dropped round half an hour later.

"Hi whack, sorry 'bout earlier like, but I thought you might fancy a drop of this" he grinned, squinting up at the barrel on his shoulder. His somewhat specialised homebrew was nearing its 'use by' date anyway — not that it would worry Ned unduly — so finding a good home for it seemed the sensible thing to do.

"Don't mind if I do me ol' whacker, don't mind if I do at all" beamed Ned, more in anticipation than mere gratitude. He longed for the simple pleasures of the Shafton Arms, but Joss' homebrew would more than suffice for the time being — and a whole barrel of the stuff too!

"I 'ad to rush in, only we left Ron on 'is own like, an' I could 'ear 'im barkin'. Thought 'e were tearin' the soddin' 'ouse apart we did. Still, it's all quiet now, like."

"'Tis an' all, whacker me ol' mate. I just 'opes 'ee

didn't piss on 'im " replied Ned, not believing a word of it. He'd have been well aware of a dog barking next door, and he'd not heard a sound — but why Joss should have to make up such a tale was beyond him. That was all water under the bridge now though, there was serious work to be done here — if old hippy features would ever get that flaming barrel down off his shoulder.

Next door a rather nervous Yttrium and Argona were being given the guided tour, whilst Ron whined at the back door to be allowed back in. He couldn't understand why Fleur had suddenly turfed him out of the cosy armchair when they'd returned home, after all, it wasn't as if he'd disgraced himself in one of the corners again — he'd learned by now that simply wasn't acceptable.

Pity really, corners of rooms are much more convenient than having to traipse outside and perform on wet grass, and it's good to have one's own personal odour about the place — it makes a certain territorial statement — but if the price of such pleasures is having one's nose rubbed in it, before being chucked out in the rain for half an hour, then one simply has to learn to adapt.

That there were visitors in the house was pretty obvious — the new smells clearly indicated that — but that usually meant a time for lots of fuss, cuddles and games and stuff, not banishment. This simply wasn't on, there was only one thing for it, he'd just have to resort to his pathetic, lonely little doggy routine — that would bring her running. As he wound up the pitiful whine to a full-scale howl, he couldn't help wondering if these visitors had brought him anything to eat.

Argona was intrigued to see an Earth biped's home, the bathroom in particular being a source of tremendous fascination. Although only just tall enough to peer over the top of the sink, she could fully appreciate its purpose, and that huge bath offered sensual delights she'd only been able to dream of these past twelve years.

Indeed, that the home was divided into clearly defined areas — each with a specific purpose such as washing, food preparation, eating, sleeping etc — was quite a quaint notion, one perhaps worth considering when they eventually returned to Strontium.

Yttrium wasn't convinced, although he could be sure that if Argona truly intended to modify their home, then modified it would be. He was more concerned with a more immediate problem, that of the howling quadruped which would shortly be allowed back in.

Sunday is usually such a quiet day in Shafton, but today was to prove the exception. It had been a far from quiet night in the pub, the flush seemingly being pulled every ten minutes, preceded by the most agonising wretching sounds from one or other of the journalists. Clearly something had upset their delicate constitution.

One by one they staggered down to breakfast, looking like death warmed up — but only ever so slightly warmed up — and even Georgie's beaming smile failed to improve their humour. The coffee pot was emptied in a matter of minutes as they tried desperately to replace some of their lost fluids, but the sound of cornflakes pouring into a bowl seemed like an avalanche of gravel into an empty oil drum — or paint kettle.

Worst affected of the trio was Morgan, which surprised Georgie not a jot — any man who ends a meal with a large port, and then goes on to neat brandy for the rest of the evening is just asking for trouble. But the speed with which he disappeared up the stairs when the eggs, bacon, sausage, mushrooms and fried bread arrived had to be seen to be believed.

In fact there were no takers at all for this sumptuous fare, not that Georgie was unduly worried — it had, after all, been paid for. The newspaper lad must have thought it was his birthday when he arrived, I mean, it's not every day you get the chance of such a breakfast — and for only fifty pence.

Mind you, he was in need of it having struggled all the way from the shop with his unusually heavy load. There was a copy of each of the Sunday publications to be delivered to the pub — and all the supplements — so he'd more than earned his sustenance.

The tabloids had splashed the story, such as it was, all over their front pages with headlines like 'MINISTRY OF SECRETS', and 'HUSH UP AT MOD'. Their pictures, in the absence of any current material, were library shots of previously unexplained UFO's and crop circles, even ET was dragged out of retirement — much to the delight of Mr Spielberg's accountant.

The broadsheets, however, restricted their reportage to a few column centimetres, some on the front page but mainly inside, preferring to print the agency story virtually verbatim until such time as their own hacks had filed their reports. By the look of the three specimens in the pub, that was likely to take rather longer than was first envisaged.

"Any sign of this Thrubwell fellow yet?" barked Morgan, tossing yet another newspaper on the floor as Georgie brought in more coffee to ease their suffering.

"Can't say as I've seen 'e yet" he replied, trying his best to sound surprised that his old mate hadn't shown up. "Per'aps 'e ain't well" he continued, "somethin' I can 'elp 'ee with, is ther?"

"Yes, there is. Either get him down here now, or tell me where he lives and I'll go to him — but I must speak with him right now, do you hear what I'm saying?"

"Well I s'pose I could go look for 'im. Might take some time though, that sort of bloke is ol' Ned, 'ee never knows wer to look — could be yer, could be ther, could be anywhere." Georgie looked innocently up at the ceiling as he waited for the penny to drop. And waited.

"Could take I hours to find 'im, an' I ain't sure I can spare the time right now, like" he continued, but Morgan's aching head still hadn't grasped the message.

"Busy place this, 'ee knows, lots to do like — still, musn't stand about talkin' all mornin', time be money — bain't?" At last he'd got through and found someone in. Three crisp £10 notes slid across the table under Morgan's trembling right hand, the heavily bloodshot eyes staring coldly into Georgie's. "Just get me Thrubwell — but get him now."

Ned may well have been a fool to go opening his mouth about his imagined encounter with flying saucers and the like, but there was no getting away from the fact that it was now turning into a very handy little earner. It was only right, therefore, that the old fool should share in the bonanza — but it had to be handled properly.

Left to his own devices, Ned would simply spout the lot to all and sundry for absolutely sod all which, given that these hacks were heavily bankrolled, would be something of a pity — to say the least. But there were bridges to mend if his relationship with Ned was to become mutually beneficial, and the proverbial olive branch would need to be delivered in person.

Armed with a bottle of twelve-year-old single malt whiskey — which would, naturally, be charged to the hacks' account anyway — Georgie jumped into his car and set off for the Olde Bakehouse.

Next door, in the Olde Brewhouse, Yttrium and Argona were languishing in a bath full of hot water and soapy bubbles, their senses soaking up the sheer luxury provided by their hosts. As the dust, grime and decaying body tissues of the last twelve years gently floated away, their skin took on the healthy glow of a newly-emerging leaf before the sun gets at it, soft, supple and bristling with energy.

Downstairs in the kitchen Fleur was rummaging through her cupboards for food to serve her guests. Tins of corned beef, Irish stew and chilli con carne — her stand-by meals making up what her mother used to call the 'War Cupboard' — were of little use to vegetarians, but right at the back of the cupboard she managed to find a couple of old, rusting tins.

They had no labels but were of the large, family size. With no way of knowing their contents she decided to open them anyway and, if they contained meat, then Ron — who was still howling pathetically outside the back door — would be in for a treat.

The contents of the first can were pineapple chunks in syrup — and still in remarkably good condition. Her guests were well able to handle fruit so this should present no problems for the pudding course, but what about the second mystery tin?

Baked beans in tomato sauce. Fine. She had guests who'd been travelling for twelve years without a decent meal, and all she could serve up was baked beans and pineapple chunks. But there was no alternative at this time on a Sunday night — other than to borrow from a neighbour, which would arouse unwelcome curiosity to say the least.

No, she'd just have to make the most of what she had. There was a little leftover cheese in the fridge and plenty of bread in the bread bin, albeit a little stale, so beans on toast it would have to be, topped with a little cheese to make it look posh.

Joss was put in charge of toast production, something even he could manage, while Fleur grated the cheese and put the beans on to warm up, before taking the spare bedding out of the airing cupboard. As everything seemed to be under control in the kitchen, she nipped upstairs to make up the bed in the guest room, leaving Joss to keep an eye on the beans as well as the toast.

The old eye-level grill was notoriously slow to heat up, so Joss took advantage of the time lag to roll another joint. With guests to entertain he would build an extra large one, for which he would need three cigarette papers, but there were only two in the pack. He had another pack somewhere, but where?

As he searched high and low for the fresh pack the ancient grill slowly came to life, terminating in the process the lives of the slices of bread beneath it. By the time Joss returned, not only was the toast well and truly cremated, the beans were also a smouldering, glutinous mass, and the entire kitchen was filled with thick, choking smoke.

By the time he reached the back door his lungs were screaming for fresh air and his eyes were streaming, so much so that he didn't notice Ron sneaking in underneath the billowing smoke. With his master battling with the cooker's controls, Ron saw little point in hanging around the kitchen waiting for scraps. There would be plenty of leftovers for him tonight, but somehow he just didn't fancy a bowl full of smouldering, crisp carbon.

There were other smells to savour tonight — strange smells he'd never experienced before — and why the hell had he been shut out anyway. There was some serious investigative work to be done here. Darting from corner to corner of the little sitting room he picked up traces of the mysterious odour, a foetid, acidic fragrance indicating the presence of a living creature — but one who's personal hygiene left rather a lot to be desired.

It couldn't be a cat, they're far too clean — besides, no cat he'd ever come across had a whiff anything like this. It couldn't be a pig, could it? Surely not. Surely they wouldn't keep a pig in the house — but then in this house nothing could be taken for granted.

Following his nose up the stairs, Ron spotted Fleur in the spare bedroom making up the bed. Should he go in, with tail wagging and adopting that ridiculous, cringing, posture she always found irresistible? He thought better of it, seeing as he'd sneaked in anyway, besides, there was still that little matter of the strange pong to get to the bottom of.

It was seeping through underneath the bathroom door but the door was shut — or was it? Pawing gently at the door, he was pleasantly surprised to find it yielding so he pawed some more. And it opened some more, revealing a room full of steam and the sounds of movement in the bath tub.

If he were ever to be listed in "Who's Who", taking a bath would certainly not feature in Ron's list of favourite pursuits. Neither could Joss lay claim to being an especially regular incumbent of that particular piece of furniture, which is why Fleur had encouraged them to play in the bath together.

They would be in there for hours sometimes, and the floor would be absolutely saturated by the time they'd finished ducking and diving in the warm suds like a pair of delinquent drakes, so Ron was slowly coming round to the idea that bath time could be fun — as long as it was a shared experience. And the signs were that there was somebody here to share it with.

Just who was the most surprised when the little black face peered over the top of the paws now resting on the edge of the bath would be hard to say. The sight confronting Ron was totally unlike anything he'd ever seen before, but they looked funsize, while for their part, Yttrium and Argona were experiencing panic levels they never knew existed.

Not even when their vehicle came under the gravitational pull of an uncharted black hole had they been so hysterical — at least then they had a vehicle which would respond to the tremendous mental effort required to extricate them — but now they were completely helpless, utterly at the mercy of this fanged beast which, even now, was clawing its way into the bath tub with them.

With an almighty splash, Ron belly-flopped into the water, making straight for Yttrium whose petrified face he now licked in greeting whilst, at the other end of the bathtub, Argona was faced with a furiously wagging tail — and the prospect of her husband being eaten alive.

Quick as a flash, the six bony digits of her right hand grasped the hairy scrotum dangling in front of her eyes and squeezed hard. With her left hand gripping the bath tap for leverage, she scrambled to her feet to try and pull the beast — which was, by now, emitting the most appalling howling noises — away from Yttrium, as Fleur came dashing into the bathroom.

The howling also alerted Ned and Leslie next door, who came rushing out into their back garden to find out what the hell was going on. Confronted with smoke billowing from his neighbours' open kitchen door, Ned raced to his greenhouse, filled a bucket with water from his rain barrel, and passed it to Leslie who, by now, had managed to clamber over the fence.

Joss' comatose form lay in the doorway, probably the most sensible place to faint when there's plenty of smoke about, and Ned was relieved to find he was still breathing — as much as he liked old Joss, the thought of mouth to mouth resuscitation with a bloke was not particularly appealing.

When they dragged him out into the garden, the cool clear air revived him sufficiently to be able to recognise his rescuers. In that peculiar, misty, half-life between consciousness and oblivion, his whereabouts and reason for being there were neither clear nor important. What did seem overwhelmingly important, however, was that he must protect Yttrium and Argona, and the only way he could that was by keeping their presence secret.

"Don't go in, man, like just don't go in" he mumbled almost incoherently as Ned cradled his head in the crook of his arm, splashing cold water into his face.

"Bain't nothin' to worry 'eeself 'bout me ol' whacker, 'tis only a bit of smoke from they ther beans — 'tis all gone now" reassured Ned, pointing at the smouldering pan Leslie was carrying from the kitchen.

Seeing the pan brought it all back, together with the awful realisation that Fleur was not going to be the least bit amused. She'd left him in charge of the only available meal for their guests and he'd blown it. He felt another faint coming on.

"Don't go in . . . danger" were the only words he managed to utter before slipping into the welcoming calm, leaving Ned to wonder what the hell he was ranting about. Well maybe the kiss of life was called for after all, but Leslie could do it.

Ned couldn't see any obvious signs of danger, but wasn't it strange that there was no sign of Fleur? And all that howling earlier, and all the lights on upstairs — just what the devil was going on? Becoming more convinced by the minute that intruders were holding Fleur hostage upstairs, he grabbed the nearest heavy implement — an axe — and stealthily made his way inside.

Finding no-one lurking in the downstairs rooms, Ned summoned up his courage and crept through the hallway with his axe raised, only to be met on the staircase by a very soggy and sorrowful Ron who, noting the old man's posture, decided to scarper, pronto, letting out a yelp as he flew past. He felt it was the least he could do to warn Fleur, in the circumstances, bravery not really being his kind of thing.

So concerned was Ned with the strange appearance and behaviour of the dog, that he was oblivious to the sound of his own door bell. It rang several times as Georgie, knowing there must be someone in if the lights were on and the telly was blaring, refused to give up.

Fearing there may be something wrong, he went around to the back of Ned's house, but could see no signs of life. In fact it wasn't until he peered over the fence and saw Leslie, apparently snogging with the prostrate Joss, that he realised there was indeed something wrong.

That Joss was a dope head was not exactly a secret around here, but to involve Leslie — and, presumably, Ned — in his narcotic pleasures was simply not on. Action had to be taken to save his old friend from becoming yet another junkie on life's scrap heap, besides, Ned would look a proper Charlie in front of the world's press if he was stoned out of his skull.

Creeping over the fence so as not to disturb the lovers, he inched his way past them and tip-toed into the kitchen in search of Ned. Quite what he was going to find he dreaded to think, but find him he must — and fast. The press wouldn't wait for ever, they had deadlines to keep and a hefty bankroll to be relieved of.

Meanwhile, completely unaware of the events below stairs, Fleur was trying to placate her terrified guests as she helped them from the bath, wrapping them in warm, fluffy, towels and assuring them that Ron was nothing more than a playful pet.

Very gently she patted their delicate skin dry, wrapping them in fresh, dry towels and leading them hand-in-hand into the bedroom to dry their hair. It was Yttrium who first spotted the mad axe man lurking in the shadows on the stairwell, and he clung to Fleur for dear life.

"Now come on, Ron's not going to hurt you" she smiled down to her little friend, turning to the stairway to shoo the dog downstairs. But the sight now confronting her was like something out of an Alfred Hitchcock horror movie, with Ned — his axe raised — frozen to the spot, transfixed by those two pairs of deep purple, almond-shaped eyes peering at him through the ballustrade.

Fleur's screams brought Georgie leaping up the stairs and, sizing up the situation in an instant, he wrenched the axe out of Ned's hand. Very carefully he sat his old friend down on the stair, but all he could get out of him was a babble of rubbish about little green men as he stared, wide-eyed, into empty space.

It was perfectly clear to Georgie now just what had caused this hallucination, and the 'sighting' of flying saucers — the same thing which was responsible for the depravity he'd witnessed in the back garden. Well enough was enough. If the ageing hippies wanted to fool around with dope that was fine by Georgie, but they weren't going to get away with wrecking the lives of others, not if he had anything to do with it.

As he turned to give Fleur a piece of his mind, his cold, icy, stare was met by the almond-shaped eyes of the little green faces now pressed up against the handrails.

chapter 10

At the Hatch End road junction, Ron Runstable was settling down for another night of total tedium.

His roster had him positioned at this point every night now for three very good reasons. First and foremost it was easy for Ruby to bring his food and flask — if the task-force commander starts falling apart for lack of nutrition, the whole flaming shooting match is in trouble.

Second on his list of priorities was toilet facilities. The little tent and chemical lavatory at the main site were perfectly adequate, but he'd noticed with regular monotony that the timing of his bodily functions seemed to be synchronised with just about every member of the MOD team.

But not perfectly synchronised. Maybe it was his age, or perhaps it had something to do with the responsibilities and worries which rested heavily on his shoulders, but the timing of his urges lagged behind those of the other sharers of this single facility by a good five minutes — by which time a not inconsiderable queue had built up in front of him.

At least in this neck of the woods he could slip behind the hedge whenever the mood took him, although Ruby had been indecently curious about his request that she bring his garden spade.

His third reason for choosing this site was its tranquility. Although it was the main — indeed, only — entrance into the site by road, very little traffic needed access to it. There were regular deliveries from Harrods, Fortnum and Mason and a host of other suppliers of essential comestibles of course, but they came during the daylight hours when one of the rookies would have to deal with them.

Guard duty at the five barred gate into the site was just as tedious but nowhere near as tranquil. There were humming and buzzing noises, and all manner of flashing lights to contend with all night long — not to mention that stomach-churning stench.

It was almost as bad down at the hamlet end of the lane, where the sounds echoed around the derelict buildings. The low, droning noises, in particular, seemed to vibrate the very earth itself, and flashing lights lit up the night sky. It was like Disney World, Heathrow Airport and a Pink Floyd concert all rolled into one.

And if that wasn't enough to put up with, there were the Fflitches. They never seemed to sleep, and anything just the teensiest bit out of the ordinary drew endless attention. They would crowd around just staring at the poor bobby on duty — not saying anything, not behaving in a manner likely to cause a breach of the peace, just staring.

Runstable only did one turn on that shift before reorganising the roster, but the sight of that kid with the penchant for sticking his big toe up his nose will live with him forever. No, there was only one place for a task-force commander to station himself, and that was as far from the front line as possible — I mean, how else could he get the peace and quiet he needed to think through all the logistical problems he faced?

Sir Gordon Bacon was also settling down for the night, having partaken of an adequate repast of Quails' Eggs, Saddle of Lamb and fresh Raspberry Mousse with his staff. As he fastened the little padlock securing the entry flap zip on his tent, he breathed a little sigh of relief. Only now could he truly relax, now that he was completely on his own.

Pouring himself a generous measure of crusted Wellington port he slipped out of his workaday clothes and into the warm, welcoming embrace of his winceyette pyjamas. Ever since his boarding school days he'd been quite incapable of sleeping in anything else — he had dozens of pairs of silk pyjamas, bought as Christmas and birthday presents and still languishing in their wrappings — but once a chap has experienced the sensual delights of winceyette next the skin, nothing else will do.

The truth of the matter is that he wore no pyjamas at all whilst at boarding school, much to the excitement of the other boys in the dormitory. He was one of life's early starters, having masturbated his way through puberty by the age of eleven and, compared with his contemporaries who were still playing at it, he appeared extremely well hung.

He would arise with great flourish — even on freezing cold mornings — displaying, in the process, the highly developed state of his genitalia. This earned him enormous respect from those less well endowed — the vast majority for the first year or two — but more importantly, it drew attention away from the deformity of his left hand.

By the time he reached the second year his fame had spread throughout the school and he was held in very high esteem, especially by the new oiks, still wet behind the ears and missing mummy like mad. Bacon was a very kind lad and would take pity on them, tousling their hair and patting their bottoms to make them feel better, so it was not altogether surprising when, on particularly dark, lonely, nights, one or other of the youngsters would creep into his bed for company.

The youngsters all wore winceyette pyjamas, the prescribed uniform for night attire, together with white towelling dressing gowns, and it was during this period of his development that he acquired the taste for winceyette next his flesh. With the dawning of his appreciation of the female form in later years, the perversions of youth were set aside forever — but not his winceyette pyjamas.

Upon his walnut travelling dressing table sat a Georgian silver box, the key to which never left the silver chain around his neck. Unlocking it, he took out his cut-throat razor, his little block of uncut cocaine and, from his collection of snorting tubes, he selected the hollow porcupine quill to deliver this night's techni-coloured dreams.

As he waited for sleep to overtake his now decelerating mind, he browsed through the preliminary findings of his team's investigations. That an extraterrestrial existence had visited the site was becoming difficult to disprove — the subsoil energy readings alone were testament to that — but what bothered him was that the readings were not sufficiently high.

From the data already amassed, together with the descriptions in the Police statements, he was as certain as he could be that the vehicle fell into the classification Omega 17. Just where these came from was far from certain, and how they were powered was even more of a mystery, although very high levels of Alpha and Gamma radiation at earlier sites strongly suggested some kind of nuclear energy as a power source.

But from all these sites much higher energy levels had been detected at the subsoil level, indicating the power they needed to generate in order to overcome Earth's gravitational force for a given size of vehicle. Calculations based on data from this site seemed to indicate that when the vehicle departed, it wasn't generating anywhere near enough power to take it out of the atmosphere.

No other sightings had been recorded in the region, so it all pointed to the probability that it was still somewhere in Central Southern England, but where? And what was it doing? It couldn't just disappear into thin air, the Laws of Physics just wouldn't allow that to happen — would they?

The Laws of Physics were certainly making their presence felt in the Olde Brewhouse — in particular the Law concerning the fate of all things which go up.

Having removed the axe from Ned's frozen grip, Georgie had himself met with something of a shock as he came face to face with Fleur's house guests. In his horror, he'd flung his arms in the air and with them went the axe. Now whilst it's perfectly permissible, under said Law, for one's arms to stay aloft — provided always that they remain attached to aforesaid party's body — this is not the case with a free range axe.

This particular Law-abiding piece of equipment, having reached the point at which its motive power could no longer sustain the battle against gravitational attraction, had indeed reversed the direction of its travels, with an irresistible force.

Now it's also held by the Laws of Physics that when an irresistible force meets an immovable object, some very interesting things begin to happen. Right again. Given that he, too, was now frozen to the spot, it's hardly surprising that the object in question — viz

Georgie's head — was totally immovable but, when the crunch came, the ensuing string of profanities was very interesting indeed.

But it certainly broke the ice. The Strontian sense of humour must be particularly wicked because the incident left our two visitors in absolute stitches. The same with Georgie, although his were of the butterfly variety, the sticking plasters being secured to his bald head by a bandage tied under his chin. This seemed to amuse our little friends even further for some reason.

You would be forgiven for thinking that such a restrictive piece of bandaging might cause something of a communication problem, especially for one with Georgie's undoubted flair for the spoken word, but not so.

In fact it was Ned who first experienced the telepathic probe. At first he thought it might be the after effects of Joss' beer, especially when his mind went totally blank.

"Yer, 'ang 'bout, what the bleedin' 'ell's goin' on yer" he muttered as the green dot appeared, probing the murky recesses of his mind and stripping his inner self bare, "me soddin' 'ead's fillin' up with green gunge. What the 'ell 'ave 'ee been puttin' in that ther beer of yorn?"

"Bain't the beer, I ain't touched a drop but I got that ther greeny stuff an' all" chipped in Leslie, becoming a little anxious about the unfolding events.

"Meee an' alll" murmured Georgie through clenched teeth, relieved to realise it wasn't the bang on the head which caused it.

"Just go with it, man" urged Joss, by now an old hand at this game. "It's cool, you'll see. Just let it, kinda like, happen."

And indeed it did happen, undoubtedly the single most impressive experience of their entire and not inconsiderable lives, as visitors from another world communicated thoughts, images, impressions and profound understanding directly into their collective psyche. For once in his life Georgie was truly speechless.

The following morning, having removed the bandage and trusting to luck that the sticking plaster would hold, Georgie greeted the journalists with his usual, beaming, smile and a full English breakfast. This time it went down well, and he just hoped it would stay down — these city types clearly didn't have the stomach for wholesome country food.

"Good morrow, Landlord" quoth Morgan almost merrily, "and do we yet have any sign of friend Thrubwell, pray?"

"Marnin' to 'ee, sir, an' I can tell 'ee I managed to track down ol' Ned last night, as promised."

"And?" asked Morgan, becoming a touch impatient.

"An' 'e says 'e'll be 'appy to 'ave a chat with 'ee like. Five 'undred quid."

"Five hundred pounds — for a chat? The man's dreaming."

"Plus extra if 'ee wants to take pictures."

"He must be out of his tiny mind, my editor would never sanction anything like that. Where is he? I want to talk to him — now."

"Five 'undred quid, that's what 'e says, an' that's 'is final offer."

"Is it indeed, well in that case we're clearly wasting our time here. I'll bid you a good day sir."

Blast. Georgie really thought they'd go for it, but he'd blown it. There was no point backing down now and offering a lower price, besides he was hatching a little scheme which, if it came off, would have them begging him for an interview with Mr Thrubwell — and for considerably more than five hundred quid.

That night, leaving Jill in charge once again, Georgie drove off in his empty van. It wasn't empty for long though. As he pulled into the long, sweeping driveway of Shafton Manor, three flashes from Ned's torch directed him to the old barn. Within minutes they'd loaded up with ladders, planks, ropes and barrel hoops and were away into the night like a pair of naughty schoolboys.

The following morning Sir Gordon was undergoing his usual mental perambulations, in preparation for stepping out of bed, unlocking the padlock and allowing his man in to dress and shave him, point him in the direction of the breakfast table, and muck out.

Their time at this site was drawing to a close. They'd gleaned all the data they could possibly require during the first eight hours on site, the remainder of their time being spent de-energising it — thereby leaving no real evidence for the hoards of enthusiastic amateurs who usually turned up in their wake.

All the other expensive kit which hummed, buzzed and flashed all day and all night had its proper scientific function, of course, but its main purpose was to provide a sop to the increasing number of Ufologists — at least they would get the impression the government was taking such matters seriously, before being told there was no scientific evidence to support their supposed sightings.

Emerging from his tent, Sir Gordon wasn't altogether surprised by the mist which had settled during the night. The atmospheric pressure had been building for several days now which, at this time of year, was almost certain to bring mist — especially in the vicinity of river valleys. It was a damned nuisance all the same, it played absolute havoc with his sinuses which, given all the junk he'd been stuffing up his nose for years, was hardly surprising.

"Right, gather roud you chabs, bording briefing" announced Sir Gordon after breakfast, and after receiving the all-clear from the officer in charge of the de-energising equipment.

"Dow we've collected all our data, there's brecious little else to keeb us here gedtlebed, so would you all brebare to break camb, blease. I shall call a bress codferedce for twelbe dood. Ady questiods? Good. Off you go thed."

It was left to his personal assistant to make the necessary announcement, through the press agency, and to prepare the statement which would be made to all those bastions of free speech who deigned to turn up, in the middle of a muddy field, in the depths of darkest Hampshire, in the mist, at two and a half hours notice.

That at least should help keep the numbers down — and, therefore, in direct proportion, the number of awkward questions Sir Gordon would have to field. With a bit of luck they might even get away with faxing a single, written statement to the agency for subsequent distribution, that way the MOD's Press Office would have to handle any queries but, for the time being, they'd have to play the game by the rules and await the response to their conference announcement.

Having finished their breakfast at the Shafton Arms, Morgan and his little team were packing their suitcases into the car when the call came through from their editor. Their journey into the back of beyond hadn't produced a single line of useable copy and, for the first time in his life, Morgan was actually considering the submission of a straight expenses claim.

Even their legitimate expenses were bad enough when

all the booze was taken into account but, without even a sniff of a real story, it would be totally impossible to indulge in a little creative accounting this time.

The fact that a press conference had been called by the MOD wallahs at the site would do little to alter this situation, but at least it would while away a little time, thereby relieving them of the need to tear off up the motorway to London. They might even be able to stretch it out long enough to avoid having to go back to the office at all today — and hadn't they spotted a rather tempting little watering hole just the other side of Hampton Magna the other day?

The prospect of a glass or two of lunch put an altogether rosier complexion on the day, but they still had a couple of hours to kill before they were due at the site. They'd been unable to glean anything of worth from the great unwashed of Shafton, but maybe the good citizens of Farthing Fflitch might be able to throw a little light on proceedings.

Having informed the entire world of the forthcoming press conference, the one person Sir Gordon's personal assistant had omitted to inform was PC Runstable. There are many qualities expected of any task-force commander worth his salt, but not even the Police manual covers the science of mind reading.

Strolling up the lane in his most blissful ignorance, Runstable carefully checked all the hedgerows for signs of forceful entry during the night. Perhaps a little chat with the young rookie at the Hatch End road block might be in order, just to keep up morale — the youngster would appreciate a friendly word from his commanding officer — then a gentle stroll back down the lane to see how the other lad was getting on.

But when he reached Hatch End all was not sweetness and light. Nick Pennington was doing his best to be polite to the rather ebullient driver of the car which, even now, was actually touching the traffic cones.

"'Ello, ello — what's all this then?" enquired Runstable in his most masterly voice.

"Press" yelled Morgan, waving his press pass around as if it were some kind of magic wand, "now would you please be so kind as to remove these blasted traffic cones, and tell this young idiot to stop messing me about."

"Press or no press, 'ee ain't got no rights comin' down this yer road, 'tis shut. Now why don't 'ee just turn roun' an' go back wer 'ee come from, eh?"

"Now look here, officer, we have every right to be here, we've been invited by the Ministry of Defence to a press conference."

"Oh ar? So wer's 'ee invite then, less 'ave a look at it."

"It's not a written invitation you thick sod, press conferences like this are announced electronically, through the proper channels. Now I insist on speaking personally with the senior officer here, fetch him at once."

"'Ee be talkin' to 'im, an' if 'ee don't get that car of yorn out the way, I be gunna run 'ee in my lad, savvy?"

Clearly unable to make any headway here, Morgan picked up his carphone and got through to the press office at the Ministry of Defence. They confirmed that a press conference had been called for twelve noon, and Morgan put Runstable on the line to hear it for himself.

"So, now will you remove these damn stupid cones and let me through?" smiled Morgan sarcastically.

"Certainly sir. PC Pennington, I 'ereby authorise 'ee to remove they cones — at twelve noon, an' not a minute before." Runstable turned on his heels, winked at Pennington, and strolled off down the lane chuckling to himself. An hour and a half spent twiddling their thumbs would teach those smartarsed buggers not to mess with a task-force commander.

When the duly appointed hour finally arrived, and the three fuming hacks had been ushered into the field, Sir Gordon rose to his feet to read the prepared press handout, standing slightly in profile to present his most photogenic aspect, and with his left hand behind his back.

"Gedtlebed, the circles id the field behide be are all there is to see, add they are dothing bore thad a hoax" he began, casting a glance in the direction of the cameraman. Over the shoulders of the assembled gathering he could see the mist beginning to clear and there, in the field on the other side of the lane, he could clearly see the most elaborate, intricate, and perfectly formed set of crop circles he'd ever clapped eyes on.

chapter 11

Frankie Fflitch must have thought all his Christmases had come together. Not only had the coppers gone from the lane, meaning he could get back to earning a living from the cattle grid, there were literally dozens of people milling about in the lane wanting to get into his fields.

Morgan must have been equally pleased with the way the previous day had finally turned out. Not only did they have a terrific scoop, but the story had been syndicated around the world, earning his paper a fortune, a fact which wasn't overlooked when he slid his expenses claim — a compelling candidate for the Booker Prize if ever there was one — under the benign gaze of his jubilant editor.

Although Frankie wasn't yet aware of it, the visitors he was about to fleece today were but the vanguard of a veritable army of punters, all heading for Farthing Fflitch. Standing in the mud at the entrance to the field, collecting £1 from anybody who wanted to inspect the circles, he felt the cold and damp striking through his feet.

If his good fortune continued, perhaps he'd be able to afford a new pair of stick-on soles this year, in time for the onset of winter. That ought to provide some respite from the cold and damp now he was getting on in years although, admittedly, they weren't as comfortable as shoes.

He noticed that, for some reason, people weren't staying very long in the field, and that many of them had scarves and handkerchiefs over their mouths and noses when they left. Perhaps they were feeling the cold, he thought, savouring the freshness of the air today.

He also noticed a couple of people picking ears of corn and slipping them into their pockets, presumably as souvenirs. At £1 an ear they were amongst the most expensive keepsakes these particular punters would ever collect — and if they thought they could sneak past Frankie without paying up, then they had another think coming.

The interest of the populace in their handiwork hadn't escaped the notice of Georgie and Ned either. And didn't it seem a pity that, with money to be made, they weren't participating in this somewhat unexpected bonanza? The original idea was to bring the press barons to the negotiating table of course — and that would surely come to pass — but in the meanwhile it seemed daft to allow those cretins in Farthing Fflitch to reap the financial harvest alone.

Of one thing they were sure — when the press finally did come calling, there would be no mention of Yttrium and Argona. They had become firm friends, and one of the basic tenets of village life is that you don't sell friends down the river. If they did, goodness only knows what would happen to the poor little buggers, but you could bet your boots it wouldn't be good.

In the meanwhile, however, there was no harm in stringing along those gullible enough to believe in the mysteries of crop circles — nor in perpetuating the stories of green spacecraft made of jelly, as that particular cat was now well and truly out of the bag anyway — and if the odd shekel or two were to find a new home as a result, then more strength to your elbow.

"Now wer can us find a couple of cornfields closer to 'ome?" thought Georgie out loud. "We be gunna need a fair ol' bit of parkin' space I reckon, an' someone canny enough to milk the buggers dry when they turns up."

"What 'bout ol' Jack Marley?" smiled Ned, "Bain't no bugger gunna get past 'e without shellin' out, not any time of the day or night — 'e can smell money comin' a mile off can ol' Jack."

It was the perfect solution. Upper Clouts Farm wasn't particularly big, but the farmhouse was easily accessible, and it had a huge concrete hardstanding outside the milking parlour. The parlour itself could be turned into a souvenir shop, and all Jack would have to do was collect money all day long.

Selling Jack the idea of making money was a bit like converting the Pope to Roman Catholicism. He even helped them design and implement their Mark 2 corn circles, the very latest models with dots and dashes around them to suggest some kind of morse code.

He couldn't help feeling a little aggrieved, however, at the loss of a big chunk of his harvest but, even with the three-way split agreed with his partners, he was certain to be more than compensated. And perhaps he'd better check his insurance policy, he didn't recall seeing any specific exclusions about damage caused by beings from another planet.

The following day punters were pouring into Shafton by their hundreds, all eager to marvel at the handiwork of their extraterrestrial brethren, and to try and work out the messages left behind. Were they messages of peace? Threats perhaps? Or were they simply interstellar graffiti?

That the visitors may require refreshment had not escaped Georgie's notice and, even with the extra bar staff he'd taken on in anticipation, it was hard to keep pace with demand. The brewery dray had delivered extra barrels of Haymaker, together with additional supplies of nuts, crisps and other nibbles, but at this rate they were unlikely to last very long.

In the kitchen, Jill was rapidly becoming sick of the sight of Chicken in the Basket, Cold Meat Platter and Ploughman's Lunches, but her temporary nausea soon evaporated when Georgie showed her the day's takings.

Well aware of the little game being played by the two old reprobates, Joss and Fleur couldn't resist taking a peek at their handiwork. Yttrium and Argona were equally keen to see it, but how could they possibly mingle with the crowd without, at the very least, getting some very curious looks? Fleur had an idea.

In the Shafton Players' props cupboard, under the stage in the village hall, were some papier-mâché masks made by the school children for last year's pantomime. The traditional 'Jack and the Beanstalk' story had been livened up a bit by the introduction of a dozen or so 'Klingons' from the planet Zarg, all played by the school children themselves and, with a bit of luck, the capes which the mums had run up for them would also be lurking about somewhere.

With a two-seater baby buggy, borrowed on the pretext that she was looking after a friend's children for a couple of days, Fleur's notion finally took shape and, much against Joss' better judgement, off they set for Upper Clouts Farm.

Yttrium, too, had his misgivings, but Argona was so

keen to grab this opportunity to observe more bipeds at close quarters, that he — like Joss — had little option but to go along with it, albeit grudgingly.

Old Jack Marley was delighted to see Joss again, it had been ages since he'd bumped into him in the pub. He recalled that Joss had been in on a round of drinks he'd had to buy once, but couldn't remember the compliment being returned.

"Still, no doubt us'll see 'ee down ther another time, eh Joss?" laughed Jack, immediately convulsing into one of his coughing fits. Instead of keeping his cigarette in the corner of his mouth, as would any normal addict when both hands are occupied, he habitually held his in the gap where one of his front teeth had been — many years earlier.

The gap was the perfect size for the brand he smoked but, whenever he laughed — which, admittedly, wasn't something he made a practice of, unless it was to emphasise a point — smoke and ash would be drawn into his bronchial apparatus, which would respond in the time-honoured fashion.

The more he coughed the deeper he had to breathe — pouring yet more coals on the fire — but never for a minute did it occur to him to remove the offending article.

"Can't beat a good cough" he wheezed, turning his head to one side and spitting on a dandelion. He would always turn his head to one side before spitting if there was a lady present, he was nothing if not a proper gentleman, and he invariably aimed his sputum at a target so as not to entirely waste it.

"Two an' two 'alves, that'll be three quid please, me ol' mate — assumin' they two be under fourteen?"

"Oh aye, whack, well under" lied Joss, forking out his cash. He'd have loved to have been able to tell him the truth about their age, but the ensuing coughing fit would surely prove terminal.

The old milking parlour was a hive of activity. Young girls who'd never even seen a corn dolly in their lives were, having had a crash course, churning the damned things out like there was no tomorrow. Georgie had insisted they wear traditional milk maid outfits, including those silly mop hats, but at the wages he was paying, they'd have been happy to dress up as pantomime cows.

Even the three legged milking stools the girls sat on were for sale — half a dozen lads in the cow sheds behind the parlour were turning them out nineteen to the dozen — but the most popular items with the punters were the ears of corn, coated with luminous paint, which glowed their eerie incandescence from the darkest bowels of the parlour.

The circles themselves were something of a disappointment from close up. That they were, indeed, perfect circles was quite apparent, as was the fact that all the corn was laying in the same direction, but the overall effect would be more appreciated from a distance and, preferably, from some way off the ground.

There were only a few takers, at £2 a head, for the ride to the top of the rickety old barn on Jack's hay bale conveyer belt, but it was hoped the tethered helium balloon, due to arrive the following day, would attract a little more interest. The weekly hire cost had been more than covered by the booking received from the BBC television crew alone and, with all the world's media screaming for more details of the affair, further bookings were inevitable.

Had Joss not known the origins of the circles he'd have sworn they were created by visitors from another planet. From the outer edge of each circle to the dots and dashes surrounding them all, the distance was far greater than any human being could jump, and it was obvious that nobody had walked between them, otherwise the corn would have been trampled. He'd have to have a word with Ned about that little question.

Argona was fascinated by the reaction of the bipeds who weren't in on the secret. It was if they truly wanted to believe in the existence of life outside their own tiny speck in the cosmos, but were afraid to accept what was statistically inevitable. Surely they didn't imagine that, in a boundless universe, containing an infinite number of celestial bodies, theirs was the only planet able to sustain living organisms? How could they support such a hypothesis?

Even though their technological development was still pretty primitive, they clearly possessed the power of rational thought — admittedly some more than others, she realised, watching Joss trying to puzzle out how the dots and dashes got there — in which case why hadn't they arrived at the only possible conclusion? But then there were those, once, who genuinely held that Strontium was flat.

"Mummy, mummy, oh look! There's a spaceman mummy, look mummy, over there — there's two of them!" yelled the little brat behind the giant candy floss, pointing. Yttrium shrank back into the buggy.

"Don't be silly, darling, it's only a mask — besides there are no such things, you know that" responded its long-suffering mother. "What we have come to witness, Tarquin, is one of mother Earth's natural phenomena, created by vortices of air. They start way up in the clouds up there — can you see the clouds, Tarquin? — and come rushing down to earth, flattening the corn. Tarquin are you listening to mummy?"

"I want a mask, mummy. Those two have got them,

why can't I have one? Oh please buy me one mummy."

"Mummy hasn't got any more pennies darling, besides, you've already got a corn dolly, and a milking stool."

"But I don't want that rubbish mummy, I want a mask. Anyway, if daddy was still living with us then you'd have lots more pennies. He'd buy me a mask. It's all your fault."

Back they went to the milking parlour in search of a mask as Joss and Fleur looked at each other. Perhaps they'd pushed their luck as far as it would go, and maybe now would be a good time to take their leave, if only they could thread this baby buggy through the hoards still pouring in.

By the time they reached the car parking area, Tarquin was throwing a wobbly as he was being securely fastened into his rear-facing child seat, in mummy's Citroen 2CV. As they passed the car, Argona couldn't resist pulling her mask a few inches away from her face, revealing to the screaming child those deep purple, almond-shaped eyes. The howling stopped in an instant, and one can but speculate on the conversation which took place on that particular journey home.

Down in Farthing Fflitch, Frankie noticed a considerable curtailment in the number of visitors over the previous day's lot, but there were queues of traffic up at Hatch End — all heading for Shafton. Just what was going on here was far from certain, but it needed investigating.

Jumping into his Land Rover, with the cattle grid bars still in the back — if anybody got stuck while he was away, they'd just have to wait — he joined the slow moving traffic until he reached Upper Clouts Farm. Parking his Land Rover in the road — snarling up the traffic good and proper — he ignored the honking horns and shaking fists of the frustrated motorists and, to their utter amazement, proceeded to shin up a huge oak tree.

Crawling out to the end of a mighty bough, he managed to get a clear view of what had taken his punters away from him. Quite how it had been created he neither knew, nor cared, but what he did know was that it was far more elaborate than the patterns in his fields.

Well if that's what the buggers wants, he thought to himself, that's what the buggers is going to get. Easing himself over the bough until he was swinging from it, he dropped the last ten feet onto the roof of the Land Rover, crawled feet first through the open window of the driver's door and was away, leaving wide-eyed, open-mouthed motorists in his wake.

Returning to Farthing Fflitch he made straight for the rickety old bridge — one of his favourite thinking spots — took out his pen knife, and whittled away at a piece of wood which vaguely resembled a trout, but which would undoubtedly make a lovely clothes peg.

His corn patterns needed to be more intricate, that much he'd already decided, but what were all those dots and dashes about? Surely people didn't prefer the patterns at Upper Clouts Farm just because they had dots and dashes did they? Why?

He thought long and hard about dots and dashes, dashes and dots, until they filled his mind, and slowly it began to dawn on him. Years ago, when he was in the Boy Scouts, they'd tried to teach him Morse Code but met with little success, it was just a jumble of dots and dashes to him.

But the Scout Master had at least managed to get him to remember three dots, three dashes and three dots by making him carve them on his stave — this, of course, being the internationally recognised SOS signal, one which the Scout Master was convinced Frankie, of all people, was going to need.

So the punters were looking for messages in the patterns, were they? He whittled furiously as his brain went into hyper-drive, trying to work out a message that would have them flocking back to Farthing Fflitch. The clothes peg, at least, was taking shape.

Relieved of his burden of responsibility, Ron Runstable was back doing what he knew best, day to day community Policing. Should duty call again at some point in the future, he'd be happy to face the rigours of high office again but, for the time being at least, his talents were needed closer to home.

But not that much closer, as it turned out, as Sergeant Roberts had been inundated with angry, and sometimes quite abusive, mobile phone calls from drivers who were anything but mobile. Thus PC Runstable had been dispatched forthwith to sort out the mess in the area around Upper Clouts Farm.

"Nar then, nar then, 'ee can't go doin' that ther 'ere" he began, approaching the camper van which was blocking the road, "this be a public 'ighway, not a picnic site."

All but one of the dozen or so New Age Travellers who'd piled out of the van had, by this time, legged it over the fence and into the corn field for free, leaving the one who'd drawn the short straw to mind the van.

Having set up his folding table and chair, the minder was busy brewing up a cup of tea to while away the time, waving two fingers at the angry drivers who remonstrated with him when they finally managed to squeeze past. At least he was until the long arm of the Law caught up with him.

"What's your trouble, grandad, somebody nicked yer pension book 'ave they?" sneered the youth as Runstable approached.

"We'll 'ave less of your lip, young fella me lad, an' I'll 'ave a look at 'ee drivin' licence an' all."

"Suppose I don't want to show it to ya? What ya gunna do then eh, grandad?"

"An' just s'pose I give 'ee a fat lip, what be 'ee gunna do 'bout that?" replied the old bobby, looking the little scrote right in the eye. "I don't know wer 'ee mates be, sonny Jim, but they ain't yer to back 'ee up. An' 'ow many of they drivers back ther do 'ee reckon'll come 'elp 'ee, eh?"

The lad got out his driving licence as Runstable wandered around the van, notebook in hand.

"Nar then, son, two bald tyres, cracked mirror and no road fund licence disc — an' that's just for starters. Magistrate over in 'ampton 'on't take too kindly to that — I reckon you'm looking at six months in the slammer, laddie."

"You pullin' my plonker or what? Ten hours community service an' 'undred quid fine, tops. That's all me mate got darn Millwall."

"Did 'e? Well 'e can think 'isself bloody lucky 'e weren't up before the beak in 'ampton. Bloody well 'anged a bloke last week — for shop liftin'. Took the poor bugger a good ten minutes to die, 'orrible to watch it was, all that kickin' an writhin'."

"Straight up, no shit?"

"Oh ther was plenty of shit, son. Ain't never seen a bloke yet go to the gallows without shittin' 'isself."

The lad searched Runstable's face for signs that he was only joking. There were none. Just that cold, steely stare any poker player would give his right arm for.

"Tell 'ee what I be gunna do, lad. I be gunna run a

PNC check on that ther van of yorn, but me radio's in the car back ther. I reckon me back'll be turned a good minute an 'a 'alf, if 'ee gets me drift."

He heard the engine start before he'd taken ten paces. Two more paces and the screeching of the tyres confirmed he need take no further action — he merely returned the grateful waves of the drivers who were, once more, travelling freely on the highways and byways of Hampshire.

chapter 12

With less than twenty four hours until his meeting with Emilia, Joss was once again becoming a nervous wreck.

The business plan concept had seemed so simple when Yttrium explained it to him, now it was just a jumble of words again. Besides, if he remembered correctly, the whole damned thing relied on his finding another use for the plastic injection moulding machines and, with all that had been going on recently, the matter had gone clean out of his head.

Realising the state his friend was getting in, Yttrium took him to one side and went through the concept again until, once more, it was beginning to make sense. But they were stuck when the time came to hang a few numbers on it because they still didn't have a product.

Even Yttrium, as clever as he was, had difficulty here because his knowledge of plastic injection moulding machines was limited to what he could glean from Joss' brain — and that was not a lot. Neither did he have much idea about the kind of product bipeds would need — or, rather, believe they needed if the right marketing tactics were used. Depression began to descend once more as stalemate loomed.

The gloom was broken by a knock on the front door, causing the Strontians to dash for the cupboard under the stairs, their now well-rehearsed procedure for such an eventuality.

"Evenin' Joss, 'ope 'ee don't mind I droppin' by unannounced like, only I was 'opin' 'ee could 'elp I with summat" began Georgie, not sure quite where to start — nor indeed whether he had come to the right quarter.

"Sure thing, whack" beamed Joss, delighted that someone seemed to value his opinion, and ushered him through to the sitting room where they were shortly joined by their little pals.

"Well 'tis to do with this yer business at Upper Clouts Farm. To be 'onest with 'ee, us can't get 'nough stuff to flog to they punters like, an' ol' Ned come up with the idea of floggin' little green flyin' saucers — like what 'e seen down Farthing Fflitch.

"Only 'ee works over Prossers like, an' we was wonderin' if 'ee'd know who us could 'ave a word with, see if us can't get 'em to knock a few out in plastic. Reckon it's a goer?"

Argona looked at Fleur, who flashed a glance at Yttrium, who smiled at Joss who, after a minute or two, finally got the message.

Long into the night Yttrium and Joss worked on the business plan, the design of the product, and what would be needed to convert the existing machinery and, by the time they hit the sack, Joss had it all down in black and white ready for presentation. He slept like a baby.

Fleur, on the other hand, didn't. Her mind had gone racing back to the days when they went to rock concerts where, if Joss was particularly flush, he would buy her a couple of fluorescent necklaces, which she sometimes used as headbands.

All she knew about them was that they were very pretty, and that you had to slap them pretty hard against something before they would begin to light up. She also recalled that the light only lasted about four or five hours, although a faint glow could sometimes be achieved after sticking it in a fridge for a while, but exactly what caused the fluorescence puzzled her all night because it would simply transform the product Joss was working on.

The following morning Yttrium was able to come up with an entire list of chemicals which, when used in the combinations given, would create the desired effect. Whether all these would be available on Earth remained to be investigated, but Joss was more than ready to find out.

By the time the BBC Television crew arrived at Upper Clouts Farm, the helium filled balloon was securely tethered, via a pulley, to Jack's tractor thirty yards away. Through the simple expedient of driving the tractor towards the pulley the balloon would rise and, by reversing the tractor's direction, it would be brought gently back to the ground.

The four-man basket was now being secured to the balloon ready for the first ascent and, when the TV crew had finished, punters would get the chance to appreciate the circles from a height of ninety feet. It would, however, be necessary to lighten their load a little before it could get airborne — about £5 a head ought to do it.

Having spent the night at the Shafton Arms, the BBC crew were wishing they hadn't sampled the Haymaker brew with quite so much gusto. It's a sneaky little ale, allowing one to savour its mellowing effects for a few pints before attacking the brain cells with a vengeance, so it's hardly surprising that headaches of gargantuan proportions have been attributed to it over the years.

And drinking plenty of strong, black coffee the following morning doesn't seem to help much either — instead it seems to trigger off a secondary fermentation in whatever grey matter managed to survive the onslaught. It was in just such a state that the crew, led by their similarly debilitated Producer, Simon Twistleton-Horne, arrived at the farm, looking for all the world like walking wounded from the battle of the Somme.

"Right you chaps" whispered Twistleton-Horne hoarsely, as much for the sake of his own head as anyone elses, "lets get the kit into the balloon and get on with it." He needed a balloon ride about as much as he needed another pint of Haymaker right now, but the Beeb needed his footage for the One O'clock News so he was just going to have to put a brave face on things.

With the camera set up, crew on board, and his dark glasses shielding his delicate eyes from the glare of the corn field, he signalled the tractor driver to move forward a few feet — slowly — to check how quickly they would rise. They didn't. He beckoned the driver to come in a little more, but still they remained motionless.

Finally, with the tractor right up to the pulley, and the rope lying slack on the ground, he hit upon the notion of unhooking one of the ballast bags from the side of the basket to lighten the load. A slight rocking motion indicated that they were now clear of the ground, but only by a few inches, so he whispered to one of his colleagues to unhook another bag.

At last the equilibrium was broken and the balloon gently rose, providing them with a splendid view of the circles which, the cameraman confirmed, were now "In the can, Simon", ready for commentary to be added at the editing stage.

One of the most fascinating aspects of ballooning is the way in which sounds from the ground can be heard with almost crystal clarity — even from several hundred feet. They'd ignored all the shouting which accompanied their take-off of course — people are always excited to see such a spectacular sight, and the presence of a television crew only heightens that excitement — besides they were recording without sound at this stage, so there was no need to ask them to keep it down.

But when he leaned over the side to signal the tractor driver to bring them down, the string of profanities heading skywards was quite alarming. Not quite as alarming, it has to be said, as the sight of the tractor driver pointing to the end of the rope — which was in his other hand, and which had been unhooked with the the bag of ballast.

Now well above the tallest trees, and rising slowly, the balloon was being gently blown on the breeze away from the farm, its basket hanging tightly underneath, and its reluctant passengers frozen with fear as they clung for dear life to the basket.

As the breeze picked up they travelled faster, which at least had the advantage of slowing their rate of ascent — but just how you got one of these things to descend was beyond the comprehension of the crew. Releasing some of the helium would undoubtedly help, and there was a valve directly above their heads, but none of them was prepared to open it — if it came out too fast they would simply crash to earth, besides, nobody wanted to let go of the basket.

And so their journey continued, way over the leafy lanes and patchwork quilt fields of Hampshire below until, lo and behold, they were over another set of crop circles — two lots in fact.

The rather plain looking ones were probably those mentioned in the release from the Press Office of the MOD, and they had been clearly labelled as hoaxes, but those on the other side of the road looked rather more interesting.

They'd been aware that they were there from the Press reports, but Twistleton-Horne's boss had decided to concentrate on the Upper Clouts Farm circles, presumably because they were more elaborate and were drawing much more popular attention — but hold on a minute, there was nothing in the Press reports about that third set of symbols.

Just beyond the original, plain, circles was a design of extremely peculiar proportions. From the air it clearly resembled the figure of a man, except that it had no arms, and it appeared almost troglodyte in origin.

The head was a lateral oval attached to a very long body, by far the greater proportion of which seemed to be taken up by two legs. In fact, looking at it from directly overhead now, it was clear that the torso wasn't much bigger than the head, but the legs were enormously long — and why no arms?

And to the right of this image were some smaller symbols — were they letters perhaps? They certainly looked like letters, indeed the word 'lop' seemed to suggest itself, or could they perhaps be initials? Or maybe something else entirely? Either way this was something that deserved looking into more closely — assuming, of course, that the basketnauts ever returned to Earth, a prospect which looked more and more unlikely with each passing minute.

Sat among the wood shavings outside his hovel, whittling away, Frankie caught sight of the balloon heading towards Farthing Fflitch and raced indoors for his shotgun. This time he'd have the bastards and no mistake, he'd teach them to come snooping on people like that.

The barrels were still full of mud and grit from the river, where he'd unexpectedly ended up the last time he intended using it — when that big green balloon flew over — but this was no time to be cleaning his gun. Shoving a couple of cartridges in, he took aim and fired — with both barrels.

While the first barrel discharged its shot fairly cleanly, the second was so choked up the explosive force had nowhere to express itself except through the weakest point. This happened to be a hairline crack on the underside of the barrel — or at least it had been a hairline crack.

Now it was a six-inch long, gaping, jagged rip, but that wasn't the only problem. The heat generated in the explosion had softened the metal sufficiently to allow both barrels to be bent upwards, so that the only possible future use for the damned thing would be as a hockey stick.

Just three inches North of Frankie's right foot, and an inch and a half East of his left, was a not inconsiderable, smouldering, hole in the ground — the final resting place of several dozen small, but extremely hot, lead pellets.

And about two hundred yards North East of that hole was another, albeit very much smaller. This one was in the fabric of the balloon, pierced by a particularly vindictive pellet whose compatriots had long since given up the ghost and fallen to earth, a trajectory now being followed by the balloon itself.

As the hiss grew louder — frightening the life out of the BBC crew — the rate of descent became more rapid, an altogether more worrying problem as the spinning earth came rushing up to welcome them home. Bracing themselves for the inevitable, the crew continued clinging desperately to the wicker basket, as a drowning man clutches at a straw.

To a man, they fully expected not to hear the fatal

crash. Not that the concept of one's feet, telescoping through the space between one's ears before the sound could register, was too awful to contemplate — they simply prayed that death would claim them before their bodies met the ground.

Gritting their teeth as the huge willow tree hurtled towards them, they heard the swishing, slashing noises of the branches as they tore what was left of the balloon's fabric to shreds, followed immediately by a bone-jarring thud and the thunderous roar of water caving in over their heads.

As the little basket bobbed up to the surface of the river, miraculously still upright, the speechless crew really didn't know whether they were still in the land of the living, or if this was, in fact, the great hereafter they'd spent a lifetime wondering about. The onset of pain, however, from twisted limbs and torn muscles, came as a welcome confirmation that the hereafter remained, for the time being, just that.

The camera, jettisoned along with all the other equipment in a futile attempt to slow the rate of descent, lay in a thousand pieces strewn across some turnip patch or other. The only thing that mattered was that they were alive to tell the tale — and what a tale they had to tell.

On hearing it, from a pay-phone alongside Twistleton-Horne's bed in Hampton General Hospital, the News Editor immediately dispatched another crew — this time in the comparative safety of a helicopter — to report on the mysterious symbols in the field overlooking Farthing Fflitch for the Six O'clock News.

After listening to Grungemould droning on and on for a full forty minutes, saying what he could have said in ten seconds — the business is sunk if we don't shed staff at a rapid rate of knots — Lady Prosser was becoming very, very depressed.

She was even coming round to his point of view, mentally preparing herself for sacrificing a few for the greater good of those remaining — but would it end there? She thought not. A downward spiral, as Sir Paul was often wont to point out, is an extremely difficult thing to turn around — "You just ask those Johnnies who fly aeroplanes for a living" he would reflect, only half in jest.

Thanking Mr Grungemould sincerely for his report, and the frankness with which he'd delivered it, she sat alone in her office, barely sipping at her stone-cold tea as she contemplated the imminent collapse of her late husband's empire — and with it, her own livelihood.

"Come in" she replied to the second knock at her door, the first merely serving to shake her from reverie. "Ah, Mr Stick" she smiled, her smile belying her total lack of enthusiasm, "do, please, take a seat. Would you care for some tea?"

"Ta very much. Er, is it alright like, if I still call you Emilia, only you said last . . ."

"I'd appreciate it if you would" interjected her Ladyship, once more warming to the hippy apparition before her.

"Oh, right. Then you can call me Joss, if you want."

"I'd like that very much. Now then, Joss, what have you to tell me about the future of Prosser Prosthetics Plc?"

Carefully unfolding the grubby, well-fingered, bits of paper he'd removed from his flower power overalls — for the umpteenth time today — he apologised for the fact that the figures weren't typed, and that there were several crossings out and spelling mistakes, before launching into the meat of his — or, rather, Yttrium's — business plan.

At the conclusion he glanced across the table, fearing that this hair-brained scheme was about to be consigned to the rubbish bin — where it probably belonged. Instead he saw a smile. It was a genuine smile, one of relief tinged with real optimism, and it was to be several minutes before either of them spoke again.

"Well, what do you think then?" he ventured, feeling a little more sure of himself now.

"Brilliant" whispered Emilia, wiping a tear from her eye, "simply brilliant. It's almost as if Sir Paul himself were guiding your thoughts." She reached for a fresh tissue and blew her nose.

"But I ain't too sure about these chemicals, like, what they cost or where to get 'em. Mebbe you could tell me who to 'ave a word with, like."

"I certainly can, and I shall arrange for my secretary to get representatives of the chemical companies with whom we do business to call on you tomorrow. Oh, by the way, do you possess a conventional business suit?"

"Well, er, no. I mean I've never 'ad the need of one, like."

"Right, well first thing tomorrow morning I'd like you to drive over to Hampton Magna — there's a car in the car park you can use until we can find you something more suitable — and get yourself one. Marks and Spencer will have plenty to choose from, just let my secretary have the receipt.

"And perhaps you'd like to use the office next door, you'll find it quite comfortable. I hope you won't mind sharing the services of my secretary for the time being, until things pick up a little, then we'll see about appointing someone solely to help you."

"Does that mean I've got the job then, like" was all he

could find to say, although he could have kicked himself as soon as he'd said it.

"I rather think it does, whack" smiled the Lady to her new Manager.

Sir Gordon Bacon never missed the Six O'clock News from the BBC. No matter where he was in the world, he would always watch the programme live — even if it meant getting up at three in the morning, and having the signal bounced off several satellites.

On this particular evening he was in his office, musing over the latest processed data from Farthing Fflitch, when the alarm on his wrist watch advised him it was time to tune in. He pressed the grey button on his desk — a colour he considered appropriate for this particular facility — and sat back in his old, comfortable, deep red leather armchair.

As the burnished walnut wall panel slid gently to the left, the picture flickered a little as the familiar signature tune heralded the headlines: 'Soaring Crime Figures', 'Record Balance of Payments Deficit', 'British Rail Blames Leaves on Line for Delays' and 'Is ET Trying to Tell Us Something ?'

The final headline accompanied images from the Farthing Fflitch site, and it was clear from the presenter's voice that the Editor's treatment of the story was likely to be somewhat tongue in cheek. It was also going to be one of those 'And finally . . .' stories which nobody takes seriously but which the viewers find amusing.

Perfect. It had been a long uphill battle through a complex bureaucratic maze, but at last his department's policy on the treatment of such stories was being observed by the BBC hierarchy.

Those at the very top of the Corporation considered themselves untouchable by Government or anybody else — and said so at every available opportunity. But Sir Gordon was well aware that the real power lay in the hands of those just a little way down the chain of command — those still aspiring to knighthoods, and who could appreciate that there was little point in alarming the populace unduly.

He awaited the report with a self-satisfied smirk, wondering what angle the reporter would seize upon to entertain the masses. The smirk was soon wiped off his face, however, when the aerial shots were screened. Even though the young reporter made light of the armless, long-legged figure which called itself 'lop', this was a development of which Sir Gordon had no knowledge whatsoever. Heads would definitely roll.

Meanwhile, totally oblivious to the whirlwind of interest now gathering momentum, Frankie whittled away outside his little hovel in Farthing Fflitch. He wondered if his advertisement really was the kind of message punters wanted to see in a corn field, and if 10p was the right price for a clothes peg.

chapter 13

Yttrium and Argona were not at all unhappy at the prospect of being left alone in the house for the morning. Having made friends with Ron, they'd soon come to realise he wasn't at all the terrible, sharp-fanged quadruped they'd feared, just a big softie who loved to play.

In fact they were quite looking forward to having the house to themselves, and they might even invite Leslie around for mid-morning coffee, a quaint little ritual they would definitely take back to Strontium.

Fleur was beside herself with excitement — her husband a Manager at last, and she was to help him choose a new suit. And by 'new', Emilia had meant brand new, not a corpse's cast-offs from a charity shop — they were going to Marks and Spencer, no less.

And to cap it all they were going in his company car. She realised it wouldn't be a new one, probably one a few years old and waiting to be sold on — but what the hell, it would be a damn sight newer than anything they'd ever had before.

Making sure Joss wore a clean shirt and underwear, and insisting that he changed his socks — even if he had only worn them a few days — for a pair without darns in them, she eventually managed to get him looking reasonably presentable before shoving him out through the front door.

The short walk to the factory was the same one he'd covered every morning for a few years now, but it seemed very different this morning. As the car park came into view they looked out for an old Sierra or Cavalier, something that was getting a bit long in the tooth for the high-mileage reps to be driving, but were a little surprised not to find one.

Not only were there no Sierras or Cavaliers, there were no cars of any description, not one. Wondering if he'd got the date wrong — but then not even Joss could misunderstand "Tomorrow morning", or could he? — he decided to go up to the secretary's office and check.

"Good morning, Mr Stick. And, you must be Mrs Stick, my name's Sarah, I'm very pleased to meet you."

"Likewise, I'm sure love, but like, please call me Fleur."

"Certainly, Fleur, thank you. Can I get you some coffee, or perhaps you prefer tea, while we wait for your car to turn up? It's only down the road being cleaned up, it won't be long."

A little ill at ease at first — the only offices they'd ever had much to do with tended to be in Police stations and the Department of Social Security, where the greeting was altogether different — Sarah's genuine warmth soon helped them feel at home.

She even introduced them to Joss' new office, explained how the telephone system worked, how he could now gain access to the computer system, what to do if he needed more tea or coffee — either for himself or for his guests, and apologised for the delay, but five clear working days were required before she could get new company credit cards for his expense account. She hoped he wouldn't be unduly inconvenienced.

"Mornin' Sarah, just brought Mr Stick's car back, keys are on yer desk" shouted the car salesman. His firm did a lot of business with Prossers, so they didn't mind valeting the odd car once in a while, as a favour. It also gave them the chance to look over any cars they fancied as trade-ins, and this one they fancied very much indeed.

As Joss took the keys from the secretary, he couldn't help noticing that it said 'Jaguar' on the key ring, and cast a quizzical look in her direction.

"It's Mr Prosser's old car, you know, the red one with his initials on it. The police took it away for examination following Mr Prosser's, er, spot of trouble, and they've only just returned it. I do hope it'll be OK for you" she smiled.

After his old three-wheeled van, then his ex Post Office mini van with its knackered gearbox, he could put up with an E Type Jaguar with personalised number plates — even if they weren't his initials. Leg room in the back seats was a little restricted, but that would be fine for his house guests. Maybe he could take them out for a spin in it, they'd like that. Yes, this would do very nicely, thank you.

Heads certainly turned as the E Type drove through Shafton, with Fleur waving nonchalantly to her friends as they sped past. But there were also admiring looks as they drove through the other villages en route to Hampton Magna, looks which said "Lucky bastards", but which really meant "Why them and not me?"

And when they parked the car in Hampton High Street, the locals thought it was a pop star's car — admittedly an ageing pop star, but anybody who drives a car like that, and dresses in flower power shirts, floral pattern bell bottoms and cuban heeled boots must be a pop star, musn't he.

The dark blue, pin striped, double breasted suit Fleur chose was the epitome of commercial convention, and the new shoes and shirt set it off a treat. But long tresses of ginger hair just didn't sit right with the new image so, after a great deal of heart searching by Fleur, and kicking and screaming by Joss, those much-loved locks were consigned to the barber's floor.

All that remained to complete the ensemble was a smart tie, but on this matter Joss insisted on having his own way. He had, after all, gone along with everything up to now — the haircut, the shoes and shirt, the anonymous looking suit, but they all robbed him of the one thing he truly owned, his sense of identity. Even the car had somebody else's initials on it.

Nipping into the public toilets, he found a cubicle which still had a bolt on the door, and changed into his new kit so that Fleur could enjoy the overall effect.

Carefully removing the sales tags, which he stowed neatly in the green Marks and Spencer carrier bag with his old clothes — together with the receipt for the secretary — he buttoned up the double-breasted jacket and tied a new, double windsor, knot in his old, floral patterned, kipper tie.

Fleur was, indeed, suitably impressed, although perhaps it would look a little less as though he'd been sick if he tucked the tie inside his jacket.

Down at Farthing Fflitch the traffic was fast becoming a nightmare. Frankie had no option but to open up one of his fields as a car park, despite the fact that he'd lose his crop — but at £2 a car for parking, then £1 a head for entry to the field with his advert in it, he wasn't complaining.

What he couldn't understand, though, was why so many people would come to see his advert — and pay him handsomely for the privilege — yet walk away without buying any clothes pegs, which were clearly on display at the gate. Maybe 10p was too much.

With more and more people pouring in all the time he was glad they didn't stay very long. They seemed a puny bunch, just like the punters who'd turned up the other day, leaving after only a few minutes with their scarves around their faces to keep out the cold. A quick turnover suited him just fine though, it would mean more in his little wooden box at the end of the day.

The problems came, however, when they wanted to leave the car park. The little lane was only just wide enough to take a car, and there were hundreds of them backed right up to Hatch End and beyond, waiting to get in.

Some, in desperation, had driven down into the hamlet seeking an escape route — Frankie had left the cattle grid bars in, he was far too busy to deal with that little enterprise as well today — but they could get no further than the old bridge before having to turn around.

And now the traffic was backed up down the lane to the hamlet, as increasingly impatient drivers began sounding their horns to vent their frustration. It was left, as usual, to PC Runstable to sort out the mess — although quite where he was going to start he didn't have a clue.

"Right then 'ee lot" he shouted, trying to make himself heard above the cacophony of car horns, "what I be gunna do is this. This lot yer be gunna 'ave to get back in that ther field" he started shooing them like wayward sheep, "while the rest of 'ee stays were 'ee be. Then I be gunna walk up to 'Atch End an' tell they buggers to stay put. When I blows me whistle, 'ee lot can get into the field an' that'll leave the lane clear.

"Then 'ee lot from the 'amlet can bugger off, followed

by 'ee lot from the field, then us'll let some more in off the main road. Right, any questions? Good. Now just be patient and wait for I to blow me whistle. Right?" With that he started off up the lane as fast as his chubby little legs would carry him, squeezing past the cars — and their irate drivers — as best he could.

There had been no questions stemming from his eloquent presentation of his plan for one very good reason. Not a single word he said was heard by anybody — he'd even had difficulty hearing himself above the din — and when they saw him simply walking away from the problem, those who'd been there the longest were going purple with rage.

The phone lines in Hampton Police Station were red hot with calls from mobile phones and, following reports of two heart attacks, an epileptic fit and the imminent, premature arrival of triplets, Sergeant Roberts had little option but to request back-up from the Regional Traffic boys.

The emergencies were evacuated by air ambulance within half an hour which just left the little problem of sorting out the gridlock of traffic, something Runstable had been dispatched to deal with hours ago. Where was he anyway, thought Roberts, as his car — with sirens blaring and lights flashing — approached the Hatch End ford.

There, at the little road junction, amidst totally snarled-up traffic, stood the rotund Constable — his face a very peculiar shade of blue as he persisted in blowing his whistle for all he was worth.

By the time Joss and Fleur reached the scene, on their way back from Hampton, the traffic was moving a little more freely — but it was still obvious that, for some reason, there were an awful lot of people wanting to go to Farthing Fflitch.

"They look kinda lost, babe" mused Fleur, "you don't suppose they're looking for Upper Clouts Farm, like, do you?"

"Bloody odd, all of 'em gerrin' lost, kid" replied the new business executive, beginning to get a little impatient at all the traffic impeding what had, up until now, been a very pleasant drive through the country. He couldn't help wondering, though, if some sod had moved the signposts.

Approaching old Jack Marley's place at last, he decided to pull in and see the state of play. Hopefully Georgie would be around, and that would give him chance to have a chat about his plastic spaceships, besides, he was also a touch curious to see how his new image would go down.

Georgie was indeed around, with a face as long as a wet week in Hayling Island, and the other thing which struck Joss was the complete absence of cars in the car park. In fact the only people around were those Georgie had taken on to make and sell all the grockle gear.

"About them plastic spaceships, whack" began Joss, buttoning up his jacket for maximum effect, " any idea 'ow many you're gunna need for starters? Only I reckon we can start knockin' 'em out next week, like." He posed alongside the E Type, waiting not only for the answer, but also for the look of sheer admiration which would surely come — if only Georgie would look at him.

"Don't reckon we be gunna need they now mate. Bain't no punters about no more, buggered off over Farthin' Fflitch 'aven't 'em? Might as well bleedin' pack up an' go 'ome at this rate" moaned Georgie, still not looking up.

"So does that mean you don't want none, then" asked the incredulous captain of industry, beginning to realise his dream was falling apart faster than a haystack in a hurricane.

The red file on Sir Gordon's desk was simply marked 'DHARINSKI'. Not the words 'Top Secret', which were hardly relevant in a department whose very existence was top secret, not even a reference number or security classification. The red files, however, never left Sir Gordon's office.

The information it contained — such as it was — wasn't new, indeed the incident occurred in 1957, but it had been in his possession for less than a year. It had come from the very heart of the Kremlin where it had lain, gathering dust for all those years, until the political climate brought an end to the cold war.

The DHARINSKI file had been among the most closely guarded data for a very good reason — the Soviets simply had no idea how to cope with the problem. Fortunately the incident had never been repeated but, had knowledge of it spread in 1957, mass panic could not have been avoided.

The town of Dharinski had simply disappeared from the face of the Earth complete with all its residents. No scorch marks or craters marked the site, no rubble or refugees remained — it was as if the town had never existed. All that remained were maps and memories, and the KGB had been ruthlessly effective in the modification of both.

The area had been sealed off, the only people allowed in being scientists in full protective clothing to shield them from the high levels of radiation, thus giving rise to rumours about a terrible nuclear accident, but they found not a single living creature — nor even the remains of one.

The previously fertile pasture land was no longer

green, it was pure white. Plant species seemed otherwise unaffected by the incident — except for a small desolate area, roughly in the centre of where the town had stood. The area in question had a definite shape to it, the shape of a creature remarkably like a squid.

Within months plants were growing in this mysterious area, strange plants which the botanists were unable to identify, but one of the most curious things about them was their inability to cope with the sun's rays. On hot, sunny days they would simply wither and appear to die, but at night they would recover.

On dark, cloudless nights the large, oval leaves would all point in the same direction — fifteen degrees above the horizon, due South of the site. There was a great deal of speculation as to just why this should be, but the time for scientific conjecture was overtaken by events.

Exactly nine months after the disappearance of Dharinski, seed heads appeared on the plants. There had been no flowers to warn of this development, they just sprang from the tips of the leaves and grew at an alarming rate, sapping the stored energy from the mother plants.

The over-exuberant botanist who examined these bizarre, squid-shaped, seed pods that morning didn't live to recount the experience. The instant he touched one he screamed, then fell to the ground writhing in agony as the tentacles engulfed his hand. Eye witnesses watched, helpless, as other seed pods took hold, sucking and squeezing until he disappeared entirely — even his protective clothing and breathing apparatus vanished.

Within two hours, with the plants at their weakest in the strong sunlight, troops with flame-throwers had arrived at the site to destroy them. The destruction was total, not even a charred crisp remained to testify to the existence of this grotesque life-form and, with the troops and scientists permanently transferred to psychiatric hospitals well North of the Arctic Circle, the file was closed.

But it was the graphic illustration of the 'squid' which Sir Gordon was now contemplating. The oval head, the long legs — admittedly not straight, as those at Farthing Fflitch appeared to be — but there was a similarity which bothered him. It bothered him a great deal.

As the E Type drove slowly back through Shafton, heads still turned and friendly hands still waved in recognition. They went unheeded.

That familiar grey mist of depression had, once again, settled on their lives, a mist through which it was difficult enough to see anything, and what they did see was tainted black. Their world had, once again been turned upside down.

But what made matters infinitely worse for Joss was that he'd tasted the high life, albeit briefly, and found the taste very much to his liking. If it hadn't been for that he'd have just put the disappointment down to sod's law, as he had on countless other occasions, and just got on with things.

The fact that Fleur was involved also added to his loss. She was the one who always stuck by him no matter what, and he'd shared his moment of glory with her. Now her dream had been shattered as well, creating a double blow for Joss — unless he could do something to turn the situation around. And fast.

If the punters had stopped going to Upper Clouts Farm, what would bring them back again? The highly elaborate circles had certainly attracted them until today, but now they'd been drawn back to Farthing Fflitch by a simple design of an armless man, according to the description Georgie had given him. Further elaboration of the circles, therefore, wouldn't appear to offer much hope.

But what if they could come up with solid evidence of Yttrium and Argona's existence? Maybe let people see the spaceship? Nobody would turn down the chance to see a genuine, inter-gallactic spaceship — and perhaps he could get the little Strontians to put in a personal appearance. That would have the punters flocking back in their droves.

And if they could actually see the spaceship, then they'd be sure to buy souvenir replicas, Prossers would be saved, and his future with the company assured. Yes, that just had to be the way forward, maybe things weren't looking so bad after all.

But hold up a minute. If he exposed Yttrium, Argona or the spaceship to the punters, wouldn't that put them at risk? People can behave like animals sometimes, pushing and shoving to get a better look or, even worse, to touch the objects they've come to see. The Strontians were only little people, and really quite delicate, so would they be able to stand up to all that jostling?

And what if the spaceship were to get damaged in some way, what would become of them then? They could stay on Earth — the house Joss would buy with his management salary would be more than big enough — but would they want to? They had friends and relatives back in Strontium, people they'd want to be with again at some future point — did Joss have the right to put them at risk?

Unbeknown to Joss, in the stony silence which accompanied his thoughts on that seemingly endless drive home, Fleur was undergoing a pretty similar thought process. She hated herself for even thinking it. But think it she did.

By the time they reached their little cottage, their

minds still in turmoil as to what they should do, it wouldn't have taken a mind reader to discover their inner thoughts — they could be read quite clearly, like the pages of a book, on their faces.

As they entered the house, knowing full well that it would be impossible to keep secrets from their little house guests, Joss was already preparing what he was going to say.

He needn't have bothered. They'd already gone.

chapter 14

"My word, Joss, what a transformation" exclaimed Lady Prosser. "I must say I am most impressed. What does your wife think about your new image?"

"She 'elped me choose it, like" was all he could manage, before escaping into the sanctuary of his new office. Fortunately Lady Prosser didn't take it as a slight, she just assumed that his new responsibilities were already weighing heavy on his shoulders. He'd soon get used to it, of that she was convinced.

Joss was far from convinced. In fact he couldn't make up his mind whether to make a clean breast of it straight away. The only customer, for the sole product on which this entire charade was based, had vanished into thin air — and the only way he could turn the situation around was to betray a very important friendship, something he'd decided he just couldn't do. Now here he was, lording it around in his own office, wearing a suit, and gazing at the E Type in the car park below.

It wasn't right, he'd have to come clean. At least if he did that, before any real damage was done, she might let him have his old job back. He'd have to pay for the suit himself, of course — but he still had the sales tags, maybe Fleur could take it back and get a refund.

Just as he was about to go and confront Lady Prosser with the truth, his phone rang.

"Hello Mr Stick, Sarah here. Your 2.30 appointment has arrived, would you like me to bring Mr Martin through to your office?"

He looked at the leather bound diary on his desk and saw that he had appointments at 2.30, 3.30 and 4.30 with reps from chemical companies. He couldn't back down now, no matter how much he wanted to, so he'd just have to continue the farce until they'd all gone. Maybe then he'd be able to have a quiet word with Lady Prosser. He no longer felt he could call her Emilia.

"Yeah, OK Sarah, bring 'im in" he muttered into the phone, "oh, er . . . please", he remembered his manners just in time.

Sarah ushered the rep into Joss' office, smiled as she made the introductions and winked over the visitor's shoulder, showing her crossed fingers to wish him luck in his first business meeting. Joss appreciated the gesture, which made him feel even more guilty that he'd let the side down, but came forward to greet the man with a warm handshake none-the-less.

After taking the orders — tea, white, with for Mr Martin, and tea, white and three withs for Joss — Sarah left them to it, pleased with the knowledge that the old firm was at last beginning to make some progress.

"I understand you've expressed interest in the products of our Chemical Lights Division" began the smartly dressed young rep, opening his shiny black leather briefcase, with his company's leaflets and brochures neatly packed inside.

Joss couldn't help noticing the enthusiasm with which this young man was going about his alloted task — flogging bottles of chemicals — and how keen he was to be of service to Prosser Prosthetics Plc. He positively bristled with the eagerness of youth and, if he could bottle that, Joss would certainly be a buyer.

For a full forty minutes — time that seemed to pass in an instant — they discussed the project Joss had in mind, a project that seemed to excite the youngster considerably more than it did Joss. Indeed some of the enthusiasm was beginning to rub off on Joss as they worked out just how to achieve the luminescence in his little spaceships and, with brochures now covering every inch of his desk, the fact that he still didn't have a customer couldn't have been further from his mind.

"So if I can just make a note of what you're going to need" announced the rep, realising that he was cutting it a bit fine to get to his next call and wanting to wind this one up, "I can then get my office to fax you a quote tomorrow morning. Let's see now, you'll need Dibutyl phthalate, Butanol,t-, Hydrogen peroxide and Dimethyl phthalate."

"That's easy for you to say" joked Joss, now quite carried away with it all, "and how soon can you deliver it, like?"

"How soon would you like us to deliver it?" responded the rep in a flash, having been programmed by his sales manager to reply to such questions with a test close question. If the customer gave a specific date he was as good as placing an order, all that was needed was a swift handshake and a signature on his order pad.

"Let's see your quote first, son" smiled Joss, realising he was being railroaded. He might not be too well versed in the chess game played daily between salesmen and their customers, but he wasn't about to be hustled by the first young smartarse to set foot in his office.

By the end of the day, having been subjected to a barrage of enthusiasm from two salesmen and an extremely effective sales lady, Joss was so hyped-up over the project he just couldn't face Lady Prosser. He realised how stupid he'd been. To allow himself to be dragged along with the emotional tide generated by these sales people was unforgiveable, and to waste their time when he had no intention of buying was equally wrong.

Even so, he still had to put the record straight with his boss, but maybe he'd feel a little less awkward about it tomorrow morning — besides, he really ought to get home and help Fleur in her search for Yttrium and Argona.

The Strontians had been with Joss and Fleur all morning. Not physically, of course; but they were fully aware of the experiences and emotions they'd been through.

They'd left the house long before Joss' thoughts had turned to how he could save his fledgeling career. They became aware of those thoughts but felt no animosity towards him — after all, it would have been totally illogical not to have considered all the options.

They were glad he had, because it demonstrated his ability to think things through to a proper conclusion, but they were deeply touched that he had felt unable to betray them. Not that they were too concerned about contact with all those bipeds — they were well able to defend themselves from far greater threats than that if they had to — but they now knew just how much their friendship meant.

Yttrium, in his own, inimitable way, had devised a plan which would not only help to get things back on the right track for Joss, it would also enable them to restock the vehicle with concentrated food supplies for their eventual return. Having two good reasons for doing something was always infinitely preferable to having only one good reason in Yttrium's view and, if two objectives could be achieved with a single plan, that was a third good reason to do it.

Argona didn't need three good reasons, one would do, so she ignored his totally logical posturing and turned her thoughts to the fun they would have, the following morning, when their activities would be discovered.

"Yer Georgie, 'tis Jack . . . Yep I knows full well what time it be me ol' mate, 'tis arf past six of a mornin' . . . Never mind 'bout all that 'ee miserable ol' bugger, juss get thy arse out of bed an' over yer a bit quick — an' bring Ned with 'ee."

From the tone of Jack's voice it didn't seem like bad news, which was just as well because Georgie needed more bad news about as much as a drowning man needs a drink of water. But when he arrived at Upper Clouts Farm, still half asleep and with Ned only half dressed, he was damned if he could see what all the fuss had been about.

"'E've flipped. 'E 'ave, 'e've bin an' bleedin well flipped" whispered Georgie as the pair of them surveyed bugger-all, "wer's 'e too anyroad?"

"Buggered if I knows" replied a bleary-eyed Ned, "an' buggered if I cares. Let's get back 'ome to bed."

"No, 'ang 'bout. Us've come all the way out yer" reasoned Georgie, "let's just see what the soft ol' git 'as to say for 'isself, shall us?"

"Marnin' lads, an' 'ell of a fine marnin' it be an' all" beamed Jack. "Just bin on the phone to they blokes at the paper, they'm comin' down yer again later on, an' I reckon us'll 'ave they punters back afore the week be out — 'ee mark ol' Jack's words."

"Oh ar, an' what makes 'ee think that then?" asked

Georgie, his senses now alert once more at the mention of punters.

"Come by yer, my sonner, an' see for 'eeself" chuckled Jack, quite beside himself at the prospect of getting back on the old gravy train.

Beyond the cornfield lay a field of turnips and another of cabbages and, following the old country saying that the finest fertiliser is the farmer's boot, Jack had made a habit of checking all his fields at first light every morning, come rain or shine.

This particular morning he'd been astounded, at first, as he faced a pristine white scene — as if a severe hoarfrost had set in. But it was far too early for that kind of weather, besides, the air around him felt pleasantly warm for the time of year.

Every single turnip was pure white, including the leaves and, as he picked one up, it just disintegrated into a fine white powder. Exactly the same had happened in his cabbage field but, as far as he could tell, no other fields in the immediate area had been affected.

"What's fink to that then, eh?" chortled Jack. "Be that gunna bring the buggers running back, or what? By the end of the week I do reckon, an' I got a fiver in me pocket what says so. Wanna take I on, do 'ee?"

"'Ow 'bout a tenner what says by sundown today" ventured Georgie, certain that a call to his mate at the BBC would see coverage on the one o'clock news. He needed to have a word with him anyway to sort out who was going to pay for the balloon, as the owner hadn't been terribly understanding about its fate.

Sure enough the one o'clock news had not only aerial footage, but expert analysis to boot. A team of scientists had been flown to the farm by helicopter, and the 'Circles Mystery Deepens' news item showed them shaking their heads in disbelief. Not only had they never seen anything like it before, they couldn't even begin to provide a logical reason for the phenomenon.

"Mr Stick, please, 'tis Mr Smith yer" announced Georgie to the secretary on the other end of the phone. It took a little while before she found Joss, but eventually Georgie was put through — to Lady Prosser's office.

"'Bout they spaceships, Joss, 'ow soon do 'ee reckon 'ee can deliver 'em?"

"'Ow soon d'ya want 'em, whack?" came the swift reply.

Replacing the phone on its hook, Joss smiled at Emilia. "Just me customer confirmin' 'is order, like" he announced proudly.

"Oh splendid, well done. Now then Joss, what was it you wanted to see me about?"

High in the beech tree overlooking the whitened fields, Yttrium beamed one of his very broadest smiles to his wife. They'd been fascinated to see the strange flying contraption which landed earlier, and which then took off again with some very puzzled bipeds on board.

But they were delighted to see, well before sundown, little vehicles full of bipeds arriving at Upper Clouts Farm. And with their own, well-stocked, vehicle now safely parked back in the river, and the dark of night descending all around them, it was time to make their way home to Joss and Fleur.

Sir Gordon didn't get wind of this development until the six o'clock news, but what he saw he didn't like — not one little bit. "How dare they" he screamed, but there was no-one in earshot. In fact there was no-one else in the building, they'd all gone scurrying back to hearth and home.

First thing in the morning he'd have someone's balls for this. How could the BBC be so irresponsible as to broadcast such a report — backed up by so called expert witnesses — before clearing it with the MOD first? And what the hell were his own blokes playing at, allowing the bloody BBC to be the first to know about it?

It was their job to know what was going on in all sensitive areas, especially one in which they themselves had been active so very recently, so one or two people were heading for a very serious, and very sudden, career adjustment. Sir Gordon was not a happy chappie.

Reaching for the solace contained in his little Georgian silver box, he considered the implications of this latest development. The similarity between the Dharinski 'squid' creatures and Farthing Fflitch's 'lop' was too close for comfort, he reflected, choosing the cold, steel tube to sooth his troubled nostrils this evening.

And the whitened fields — the apparent draining of nutrients from two entire crops — just a few short miles from where 'lop' had been sighted — bore uncomfortable similarities with Dharinski, he reflected, taking out the razor.

He remembered concluding that whatever had caused the circles in Farthing Fflitch must still be in Central Southern England, but that the bastards were so close — even while he and his team were at the site — and still remained undetected, well that was just too awful to contemplate. But contemplate it he did, as the needle-sharp crystals hit the soft, raw tissue of his left nostril, exploding into an icy fireball.

And now they were on the move again, he realised, reaching for a Kleenex to wipe away the blood from the end of his nose. If they had the ability to simply drain two entire fields, in the middle of the night, a fact which remained undiscovered until some straw-sucking bumpkin happened to stumble across it the next morning, what other capabilities did they have?

By the time he'd wiped the blood from his right nostril, visions of squid-like creatures — armies of them marching unopposed across the length and breadth of the British Isles — filled his reeling head. He reached for his Dictaphone.

"Memo to K, from B" he began, very slowly and very deliberately. "I want this faxed through to him in the morning, and please make sure you do it first thing, Miss Cashcoin, it's very urgent. Text reads: Severe weather forecast. Storm imminent. Prepare for major — repeat major — damage limitation exercise. Immediate readiness. Bring heaters, blankets and thermometers. Confirm receipt. Ends."

Sir Anthony Kingsley, Chief of the Defence Staff, would know precisely what he meant, and wouldn't even think about querying it, even though he'd requested thermometers. Heaters — flame-throwing tanks and armoured personnel carriers — wouldn't present any problems, and neither would the squadron of Harrier Jump Jets, the crews of which were highly trained in the none too delicate art of blanket bombing, the systematic annihilation of everything and everybody within the target zone.

Thermometers, however, would need the specific approval of the Prime Minister. These short-range, tactical, thermonuclear devices — known as Hot Lances to the hand-picked few aware of their existence — could be armed and ready at a moment's notice, but only upon receipt of a specific code word, known only to the Prime Minister, and written on a piece of paper, in a sealed envelope, which was secured in a safe, in the custody of the Officer responsible for their deployment.

How quaint, and how terribly British, thought Sir

Gordon, that the most destructive force known to mankind, itself the product of years of technological development, and which could only be fired and guided thanks to the wizardry of modern computer science, depended on a piece of paper and a telephone call before it could be unleashed. He wondered whether the code word would have to be in triplicate, with two sheets of finest MOD carbon paper between the pages.

He also allowed his mind to roam over the question of just what that code word might be. Words like 'Holocaust' and 'Armageddon' were maybe a touch too emotive, apart from which the PM was likely to forget them in the heat of the moment — and they certainly wouldn't be written in the back of the PM's diary.

No, it would have to be a word of personal significance to the PM, something he could remember easily — his wife's name, perhaps — but then the consequences of a crossed line, when the PM thought he was addressing his wife, didn't bear thinking about.

Then again, what would happen were the PM suddenly to turn up his toes in the middle of the night? It could well be at a crucial time — undoubtedly so for the PM — but what about the rest of us who need to get on with it?

And what would be the reaction of a PM from a different political persuasion — would he or she ban nuclear weapons in their entirety? Concluding that the whole damn business was far too risky to be left to politicians, Sir Gordon gently nodded off in his comfortable, old, leather chair.

Yttrium and Argona were far less comfortable on their cross-country trudge back to the Olde Brewhouse. It was clearly unwise to use roads on which biped vehicles travel, and navigation through dark fields and woodland, on foot, was far from easy.

They could see the magnetic force lines running North to South and get a fix on those, but this particular area was simply criss-crossed with other, similar, energy lines — the direction of which bore no resemblance to the cardinal points of the compass.

It was Yttrium's insistence on following one of these that had brought them into the darkest depths of the woodland, a place where creatures of the night abound and a thousand eyes observe each single movement.

Well, a thousand and one to be precise. An old, one-eyed, dog fox was out on his nightly patrol, scavenging an earthworm here, a frog there, and maybe the odd bit of carrion left over from somebody else's meal. He'd lost his eye in a fight with a badger several months earlier, a senseless squabble over the silliest thing.

It had been a particularly wet night, and he was simply looking for a hole to doss down in as the sun started coming up, when suddenly he came face to face with the most gruesome, aggressive old brock he'd ever had the misfortune to clap eyes on — just as it was coming out of the same hole to have a pee.

"Sorry pal, didn't know this one was taken, I'll just back out of here and find another one. Hope I haven't put you to any trouble" he'd said, in all sincerity, crawling apologetically out of the hole.

Now old brock must have had a bad night, because he was in no mood to be messed with, and foxes were not his favourite kind of people. Foxes who try and break into other chap's setts were the worst kind of all — but a talking fox was more than he could take at this time of a morning.

It had been a very painful lesson for old reynard, one he'd never forget, and from now on he'd keep his mouth well and truly shut. Which is precisely what he proposed to do regarding these two strange creatures bearing down on him now.

Very slowly he lowered his body to the ground, bringing his head down between his outstretched front paws as he lay, quite motionless, hoping not to be seen. He'd have probably got away with it had it not been for the spider, which happened to choose that precise moment to descend on its gossamer thread, landing on his nose.

The shock sent him tearing through the undergrowth like a greyhound with its tail on fire, frightening the life out of Yttrium who was just feet away from the animal when it took off. Quickly noting the fox's bearing, Yttrium raced off in precisely the opposite direction, with Argona hot on his heels until, almost breathless, they reached the edge of the woods.

There, in the valley below, nestled the sleepy village of Shafton, and never were they more pleased to see the smoke gently rising from the little brick chimney, atop the thatch of the Olde Brewhouse.

And never were Joss and Fleur more pleased to see their little friends, as dirty and bedraggled as they may be, and to be able to thank them for their help.

As Fleur planted a kiss on Yttrium's cheek, he hid his face in his little hands and turned a very deep shade of green.

Yttrium was blushing.

chapter 15

With the punters now flocking back to Upper Clouts Farm in their droves, Ned's partners were, once again, as happy as pigs in muck.

But, as his old granfer was prone to say, "Money don't bring 'appiness". Not that his granfer ever had any first hand experience of the truth of that worthy maxim, most of his money, like Ned's, ended up in the urinal at the Shafton Arms.

Even so, Ned could appreciate the sentiment behind it, especially after the events of the last few days. One minute Jack and Georgie were on top of the world, next minute they were as miserable as sin. He just couldn't keep up with it all.

What was needed here was a little stability. Very few things would shift Ned from his stable temperament — admittedly the thought of all that money coming his way had caused a mild flutter of excitement, but he'd believe it only when he saw it in his hand. And so should they, if they had any sense.

But common sense seemed to have flown out of the window, as Jack and Georgie tore around like headless chickens, re-hiring the same people they'd sacked only two days earlier. The only way to bring some stability into their lives would be to ensure, if it were possible, a steady flow of punters into the farm.

That, in turn, meant keeping the buggers away from Farthing Fflitch, and keeping an eye on what Frankie was up to would be an important part of that.

So, having hammered in the last nail in his 'SHAFTON SPACEPORT' sign across the farm entrance, he got astride his old bike and pedalled off to find out what was happening.

It was as quiet as the grave, except for a tent, pitched alongside a large estate car and a van, in the field containing the elaborate circles he'd created with Georgie. He watched for several minutes as three diminutive Japanese gentlemen unloaded some very odd looking kit from the van. Finally his curiosity got the better of him, so he went in to investigate.

"Marnin' lads, 'ow be gettin' on then?"

"Cow be getting on what, pliss?"

"No, not cow, bain't no cows roun' yer 'ee dafty ol' bugger, what I said were — 'ow be gettin' on?"

"Pliss?"

"Cor bloody 'ell, don't 'ee savvy English then? All as I be askin' is — 'ow are you?"

"Ah, so! How are you, old chap? Ah, velly good. I are velly fine, thank you, old chap. And how are you?"

"Alright I s'pose. What you buggers doin' yer anyroad?"

"Pliss? What is buggers?"

"You lot, all you buggers, what be doin' yer?"

"I is buggers? Excuse pliss." The confused visitor stepped inside the tent, emerging a few seconds later sporting his Japanese/English dictionary and a big, polite smile.

The smile faded rather rapidly, however, when he eventually found the Japanese translation of the word. Bowing very politely, he clenched his buttocks together as he stepped, backwards, into the tent, warning his colleagues about the English arse bandit lurking outside.

The leader of the little expedition spoke excellent English, albeit with a somewhat incongruous American accent, and was well aware of the little idiosyncrasies in colloquial English. Which was just as well, as Ned was about to be dispatched with a rather large carrot inserted where the sun doesn't shine.

It transpired that they were a film crew, sent here by one of the Japanese television companies to report on the mysterious crop circles in Southern England.

They'd brought an entire array of scientific instruments with them, together with satellite dishes to enable them to beam live pictures back home instantly, should the occasion arise.

In the Japanese culture crime is a rarity — they are far too disciplined a people to tolerate such anti-social behaviour. Therefore, compared with their American and European counterparts, the media have relatively little with which to feed the insatiably curious minds of the Japanese people.

Anyone who has seen their 'Endurance' television show will be aware of the lengths to which they will go in order to secure audience ratings, but anything connected with unsolved mystery is even more compulsive viewing for the average Japanese.

This crew had a virtually limitless budget and open-dated return airline tickets but, in return, they were expected to come up with the goods. Failure isn't a word which translates easily into the Japanese language, and is something their masters don't tolerate. Just as a Samurai's sword is reputed never to return to its scabbard without having drawn blood, so is a television crew unable to return to its studio without having drawn a sizeable audience.

Ned was quite fascinated with the crew, and all their equipment, but he very soon realised that others would be equally fascinated. That could draw the crowds away from Upper Clouts Farm again if word got out, so his thoughts soon turned to how he could get rid of them.

"Sir Anthony Kingsley for you, Sir Gordon, on the scrambled line" announced the secretary over the intercom.

"Morning Anthony, I trust I find you well?"

"Fine fettle thank you. Got your fax twenty minutes ago and we are on Immediate Deployment Standby. Harrier crews have assembled at RAF Yeovilton, and the convoys of land-based equipment and personnel are heading for Nether Wallop and Arborfield as we speak. ETA three hours. We'll await further instructions. Slight hitch on the Hot Lances though, I'm afraid. PM wants more details before he'll sanction. Can you deal with that from your end?"

"Roger, Anthony, leave that one with me."

As he prepared to mount his bike for the long drag back up Farthing Fflitch Lane, Ned spotted Frankie's Land Rover towing yet another hapless motorist off the cattle grid towards the hamlet. But there were two more waiting to cross as well, so why should so many people be wanting to go down there for goodness sake? He'd have to find out.

Turning his bike around, he coasted down the lane — only to find no fewer than a dozen cars parked wherever their owners could squeeze them in. Several had parked very precariously right on the river bank, but the interesting thing was that all the cars still had their wheels on — in fact they were remarkably intact.

That could only mean one thing — that they were

there under Frankie's protection. But why? There were no reports of crop circles down here that Ned had heard of, indeed there were no sodding crops to put circles in, so what the hell was going on?

The answer was to be found along the river bank, where wooden pegs marked out the areas which anglers could choose. They were all priced differently, those from which greater success had been achieved in the past fetching more than the less popular swims. But even these were beginning to fill up now.

Fascinated by all the expensive kit these blokes had brought with them, Ned watched as an angler tied a different hook on his line. The hook was really quite tiny, and bound to it was a little fluffy brown feather with green spots on it. It wasn't from any bird Ned recognised, but it was very pretty all the same.

There were no lead weights or floats on the line, the way Ned used to fish when he was a lad, instead the angler cast what he hoped would look like a fly from a trout's eye view then, rather than let it sink under the water, he kept flipping his rod and pulling on his line to create the impression of a fly dancing on the water.

All the other anglers were doing the same, but without much luck thus far, so Ned wandered a little further down the river bank. Under the old willow tree sat a stout, elderly gentleman wearing a Tweed jacket and matching hat. In the hat band were inserted literally dozens of different coloured flies, held in by the barbs on the end of the little hooks.

He had a long, tubular net which stretched well down into the river, secured to the river bank by a peg hammered into the ground and, judging by the activity down at the wet end of the net, he'd already put one or two decent-sized catches in there for safe-keeping.

And it looked as though their grandad was about to

join them. As the angler's fly danced ever-so-lightly over the surface of the river, there was an almighty splash as the luckless trout threw himself at his breakfast. The angler struck quickly, locking his reel and whipping the rod backwards to sink the hook into the soft flesh of matey's mouth.

Well and truly hooked, and not liking it one little bit, matey dived for the weeds on the far side of the river. The angler knew that if he kept the line taut it would break, so he had to play it out a little to avoid this. But not too much, because if he let his prey reach the weeds he'd soon have the line snagged up in there.

Pulling his rod sharply to the left to head matey away from the nasties, he managed to reel in a bit more line — but this chap wasn't going to give in without a fight. For a full twenty minutes the battle of wills persisted, as an enthralled Ned simply stood and watched, but eventually the might of man and his technology triumphed over the primeval survival instinct.

Beaten and close to exhaustion the trout was finally reeled into the landing net, then gently lifted onto the river bank. Excited anglers, who'd watched the fight with keen interest, each drawing his own vicarious pleasure from the spectacle, gathered around as the hook was deftly removed and the catch weighed.

Fifteen pounds and two ounces, a record for a brown trout in this stretch of river, and a tale which would be told over many a pint of beer for years to come. With seeming resignation the trout was slipped quietly into the keep net to join his pals, there to await his fate while the victor, once again, cast his fly on the water.

"Took 'ee long 'nough to come back, 'aven't it Ned Thrubwell?" screeched the voice from way up in the willow tree. Ned looked up but could see nobody, which wasn't surprising as Fenella was already shinning down the other side of the trunk.

"Yer I be, 'ee ol' bugger" cooed the toothless crone seductively, peeping around the tree trunk, "ready, willin' an' able me ol' darlin'. Remember I?"

"Fenella? Be that Fenella?" asked Ned timidly.

"It be an' all" she replied coyly, stepping out from behind the tree and doing a little twirl for his delight, stumbling over a tree root in the process.

"What the bleedin' 'ell 'ave 'appened to 'ee?" he asked incredulously, staring in horror at the sunken, hollow cheeks, the dry, lifeless grey hair which hung from her head like old, weather-beaten straw, and the long, twisted, blackened toenails sprouting from her filthy, bare feet.

"Bugger all" she replied with a broad smile, displaying a healthy set of gums, "bin savin' meself for 'ee, 'aven't I? 'Ee just 'ang on ther a minute, got summink to show 'ee."

Ned could hardly wait. Anything she'd have to show him wouldn't be fit for human eyes, that's for sure. Probably the putrefying remains of a slug in a matchbox, that was the kind of thing she'd do when they were kids — anything to get attention. But at least she had a certain nubile quality to her in those days, and wasn't averse to putting it about a bit.

A little twinkle came to his eye as he remembered, with great fondness, those heady days before the war. The long hot summers when they'd play in the hay ricks — you show me yours and I'll show you mine. She'd even let him 'do' her once, his first ever sexual encounter. The whole thing was over in less than two minutes, which was just as well because he couldn't hold his breath any longer. By hell she stank.

And time had certainly not done her any favours.

Ned wasn't usually one to be squeamish, especially where women were concerned, but even he couldn't fancy that now, not even after a skinful of Haymaker and with a bag over her head. Perhaps he'd better just slide away quietly while she wasn't around.

"'Ee can turn roun' now, darlin'", cooed the bashful little voice behind him, "I be ready for 'ee".

"What the . . ." Ned was dumbfounded. The vision in grey now confronting him had tears in her eyes, and bright red lipstick hurriedly smeared across her mouth, giving the impression of a sad, drunken clown. The old grey dress she wore had once been pure white, and the tattered head dress, with faded flowers lovingly embroidered by hand, bore the remnants of what had once been a veil of fine lace.

In the palm of her right hand was a brass ring which she sheepishly offered up to Ned, indicating the fifth finger of her left hand as a suitable place to park it. Vicars and church bells weren't part of the Farthing Fflitch way of life, but such momentous occasions could hardly be allowed to pass without due ceremony.

"What the 'ell be goin' on yer then?" yelled Frankie, incensed that a marriage should be taking place without his knowledge, "an' who be this bugger — bain't one of us that's for certain sure".

As head of the family, he wasn't about to let the code of the Fflitches — handed down through generation after generation — be violated now. The chances of alien DNA entering the bloodline through Fenella were pretty remote, but that wasn't the point. A Fflitch woman was Fflitch property, not the mere plaything of any randy old bastard who fancied his chances, no matter how alluring she may be.

It didn't take Ned long to get back on his bike — he didn't even stop to put his bicycle clips on — and he was away up the lane as if his life depended on it. It probably did, Frankie wasn't a bloke to be messed with.

With his arm around his sobbing cousin, Frankie led her back to her little hovel, a twinkle in his eye, and the stirrings of compassion aflame in his trousers.

Safely back at the Shafton Arms, Ned was recounting his lucky escape to Georgie over a mug of Haymaker. Georgie had never had the pleasure of making Fenella's acquaintance but, from what Ron Runstable had told him about her and the meths bottle, and now this little episode, he'd like to keep it that way.

He also went over the story of the Japanese television crew, and how important it was to come up with an idea to see the buggers off. Georgie agreed. So the little sods had come here looking for the answers to the corn circle mystery had they? And they'd just love it to be something to do with flying saucers, wouldn't they? There'd be millions of the little buggers back home, just glued to their sets if they came up with something, wouldn't there? Georgie could smell money.

"'Ee just come 'long with I, me ol' mate, I got an idea" whispered Georgie with a wink, leading Ned out into the back yard. "What's think of 'ee then" he asked, pointing out a fibreglass fishpond he'd been meaning to use in the beer garden.

"So what? Don't look much like no flyin' saucer to I, an' don't forget, I seen one ain't I?" boasted Ned.

"Ar, like jelly, 'ee said 'twere, right? All green an' glowin' like. Well 'ow about if we fills that un ther with green jelly, lets it set, then turns it out? Reckon that idea, do 'ee?" giggled Georgie.

"Oh ar. An' if us shoves a lamp up it, like, then the

bugger'll glow alright, 'on't 'er?" giggled Ned, the idea growing and taking shape as he spoke.

That afternoon the pair of them went shopping in Hampton. They cleared the entire stock of greengage jelly from all three supermarkets, bought a packet of tinfoil, a gallon of paraffin, and a new wick for the lamp Ned had nicked from the roadworks on the Hampton Road years ago. He knew he'd find a use for it one day.

Measuring his trailer to make sure it would take the turned-out jelly spaceship, Georgie set about boiling gallons and gallons of water as Ned started breaking up the bits of jelly, to help dissolve it quickly. He lined the inside of the fibreglass pond with a thin layer of tractor axle grease, then greased the outside of a plastic bucket, which they'd stick in the middle until the jelly set, creating space for the lamp.

As the jelly began to cool and thicken, they tossed in handfuls of small pieces of tinfoil, which would reflect the glow from the lamp in a thousand different directions. While they waited for it to finally set, they removed the red glass from the road lamp, and replaced it with the bottom of a green plastic bottle.

Placing the baseboard on top of the pond, once the jelly was well and truly set and the bucket removed, they heaved it over and — extremely carefully — lifted the pond clear. Their handiwork quivered magnificently as the pair looked on, giggling away like a pair of adolescent schoolgirls. And, once the lamp was inserted through the hole in the bottom of the baseboard, the effect was quite spectacular, even from close quarters.

Removing the lamp before loading the thing onto Georgie's trailer, a large tarpaulin sheet was roped over the top. When they reached the field adjacent to the television crew's camp, the trailer had to be pulled by hand to its final resting place so as not to wake them up, but the constant sniggering of the two old pranksters could easily have given the game away.

Finally, with the trailer's sides removed and the lamp flickering beautifully in the breeze, the wobbling spaceship appeared for all the world to be hovering purposefully above the gently swaying corn.

The sound of a child's humming top, recorded on a looped tape and amplified through twin speakers slung below the trailer, droned eerily across the field as Georgie marched off towards the tent — to negotiate his fee for bringing this amazing new development to their attention.

Returning from the scene of a domestic argument, and looking forward to his steak and kidney pud, PC Runstable was grumbling to himself about the waste of Police time such incidents caused. There was invariably bugger-all he could do when he got there — unless of course somebody had a bread knife protruding from their neck — and more often than not the protagonists were kissing and making up by the time he arrived.

He spotted the apparition through the gate as he drove past, but carried on. He'd had enough grief as a result of his last report, thank you very much — besides, steak and kidney pud was beckoning and he wasn't about to miss out on that again.

Curiosity is a dangerous beast — consider what it did to the cat — and once it gets hold the victim has as much chance as a trout on a hook. Unable to resist the irresistible, Runstable turned back for a second peep. After all, he didn't have to report it, nobody would know he'd seen it, would they?

But when he got out of his car, heard the humming and saw the strange circles this thing had obviously created, his sense of duty got the better of him.

"Sir Gordon, sorry to wake you, sir, but I thought you ought to be aware of a UFO sighting just in from the Hampshire Constabulary HQ in Winchester."

"Anthony? Gordon. Mobilise. Immediate."

chapter 16

Yttrium and Argona were not the first Strontians to visit Earth — not by a long chalk.

The Central Pool of Consciousness is an immensely powerful, living organism, developed many thousands of years ago when Strontians first started to roam the universe, the initial concept being that of a 'Space Traffic Control' system, combined with a message relay service.

As individual telepathy gradually grew stronger and more reliable, the gargantuan telepathic power of the CPC service became all but redundant — until it was discovered that not only had the system been faithfully recording telepathic images ever since its inception, but that they could also be replayed on demand centuries later.

The system's capacity is virtually infinite, limited only by the imagination of those who use it but, without doubt, the archive facility is by far its most popular function.

Some of the earliest images from our own tiny speck in the universe show very elderly Strontians — it took more than two hundred years to get here in those days — instructing natives in the construction and use of pyramids.

Subsequent images show that the exercise was a complete waste of time, the sole use found for them being that of funeral chambers for the leading families — which is a bit like giving a mainframe computer system to a baboon, who undergoes an intellectual quantum leap by learning how to play noughts and crosses, then chucks the thing away.

But some of the most interesting images came from a small group of Strontians who never made it back home. Although vehicle speed had improved dramatically by this time, it was, sadly, at the expense of reliability — which was the undoing of this particular group of three males.

Stranded in dense forest, they were reduced to hunting small animals for meat, once the fruit season had past, and using their skins for protection against the bitter cold of the winter. Their attempts to befriend the natives came to nought, the relatively few sightings of them giving rise to the countless legends of fairies, pixies, elves and goblins which have populated bedtime stories around these parts for many a long year.

Indeed, when one of them was hunted down and killed, his remains were buried in a natural clearing in the forest, a roughly hewn wooden stake driven through his heart marking the spot. The stave not only took root, it eventually grew to be the tallest tree for miles around, adding further fuel to the legends of magic and mystery surrounding these little people.

It wasn't until a year or two later that two girls from the village — twin sisters from a family of pork salters — met and fell in love with the two survivors. Cast out by their family, the girls set up home with their 'goblins' in a small clearing, by a well-stocked trout river — taking the name Fflitch, a side of the Bacon family nobody wanted to know.

Their children resembled their mothers more than their fathers, although the almond-shaped eyes were inherited — with a pink tinge — as were the six digits but, curiously, only on the left hand. They also inherited something which, to this day, they take for granted — but which, if used properly, could have dramatically changed the world we live in.

They don't even have a name for it, but they instinctively know when one of the family is in danger — and often before the danger has manifested itself.

Sadly, however, their sixth sense has largely been allowed to fall into disuse. Occasionally one of the family will entertain the kids with Tarot cards or a crystal ball, and the reading of tea leaves was always highly popular — until the advent of tea bags demoted that particular skill to the rubbish heap.

The legacy left by their Strontian forbears remains for any who have the desire to develop it, but as for the marooned space travellers themselves, they met a particularly nasty end when the Bacon family finally caught up with them. Indeed their final, and most horrific, image is of their private parts being nailed to an oak tree, alongside a blood-spattered, rusty, medieval bacon slicer.

This is as far as images from the CPC system take us, but research among the dusty records in the Hampshire County Archive in Winchester has, eventually, borne fruit.

There are any number of references to *"Fflitche. That vyle, incestuous grouppe of people, taykinge living from the lande, their dwellynges made of mudde."* They come to prominence, however, in records of the early eighteenth century when Bishop Trelawney pontificated in Winchester. He suffered all manner of problems with common folk stealing deer from the Church-owned forests in which they eked out their meagre existence, so employed a most vigorous and feared Steward, one Dr Herne.

A wily character, Herne employed the services of selected poachers to act as gamekeepers — reckoning they would know all the tricks, as well as the folk who were using them. He rewarded them well for betraying their fellows, many of whom were hanged in chains for their crimes and, in the case of Ferdinand Fflitch the reward was the toll revenue, in perpetuity, for crossings of the bridge.

The toll was set at one farthing which, as it was the only crossing for miles at the time, gave the family a reasonable income. They were able to replace their mud huts and bracken-lined shelters with stone cottages and, as Dr Herne's pleasure increased with each villain hanged, so did the Bishop's gifts.

The freehold of the land on which their houses stood was particularly well received. It was followed shortly afterwards by the conviction of six of Shafton's finest young men for deer stealing, for which the Fflitches were awarded the right of Piscary — a seemingly pointless gift as they'd been helping themselves to fresh trout and salmon as long as anyone could remember — in fact, whenever they grew tired of the endless venison.

We next find the Fflitch name cropping up towards the end of that century, when one Felicity Fflitch appears in the list of Under Stairs Servants of the elderly widower, Ebeneezer Fitzherbert-Smythe, Lord of the Manor of Huntinghurst.

Quite what she did Under Stairs isn't clear from the archives, but her marriage to Lord Fitzherbert-Smythe in November 1793, followed by the birth of a son in January 1794 and the death of her husband in March of the same year, are a matter of public record.

Public Records Offices may be dry, dusty and seemingly lifeless places to while away a few hours, but the skeletal remains of days gone by can provide a fascinating glimpse of life's little twists, and a colourful insight into the flesh and blood reality of the day.

Whether it was the fickle finger of fate, yet again inserting its bony digit into the affairs of man, or whether it was due to that mysterious attraction which has bound certain families ever since Oedipus was a mummy's boy is far from clear. What is clear, however, is that Lord Fitzherbert-Smythe's death bed was never allowed to go cold.

By Christmas in that same year the Lady of the Manor had another mouth to feed, and another husband, whom she married on Michaelmas Day amid the hustle and bustle of the hiring fair. One can picture, perhaps, the crowd of itinerant farm labourers flexing their muscles outside the Rose & Crown — open all day for such fairs — while farmers bid peanuts for their services for the coming year.

It would be a time of great celebration, with the smells of hog roasts and the sounds of cock-fighting filling the market square, already brimming with fresh fruit and vegetables, bottles and jars of every preserve imaginable as the town and country folk mingled, stocking their larders for the forthcoming winter.

Amidst all this the Church bells rang out, heralding the arrival of the bride and groom. The Lady of the Manor, heavily with child, and the new Lord of the Manor, Josiah Bacon — Sir Gordon's Great-great-great-grandfather — would have cut quite a dash as they paraded through the market place, not to mention the vicious tongues they would have set wagging.

But Sir Gordon's interests lay not in his family's roots, nor indeed in history of any kind other than that with a military significance, and thus he remained blissfully unaware of his links with the Fflitches.

The Strontian gift of the sixth sense, however, still lingered in his genetic code. Transmuted through generations of neglect, little of the original power remained, and what did survive was simply assumed to be part of his own, inestimable brilliance.

His talent for extremely profound, multi-dimensional, abstract assessment had stood him in very good stead over the years, indeed it had brought him to the position of authority and influence he now enjoyed, but his weakness for the crystallised essence of the coca plant was warping his ability a touch.

Downtown Tokyo was in the midst of its smog-laden rush hour when the first television pictures filtered through, snarling up the traffic quite nicely as drivers pulled over — or simply stopped dead in their tracks.

Crowds quickly gathered under the giant television screens of the shopping malls, and around the shop windows of the electrical stores, while others switched on their tiny portables for a better view.

At home, Japanese housewives in their millions dropped everything to stare in amazement at the incredible scenes, beamed live from Southern England. So this was the mysterious creator of the crop circles, discovered at last — exclusively — by those brave young men for whom national pride meant more than personal safety.

They would go down in the annals of Japanese history with the all-time greats — Sony, Toshiba, Nissan, Toyota — and, if they ever got out of there alive, a welcome fit for heroes would bring the entire nation out onto the streets for their return.

Never had the Japanese predilection for staring at inanimate objects been more thoroughly satiated. For three hours they gaped in sheer bewilderment as a pile of greengage jelly, with an old roadworks lamp stuck up it, wobbled away in the dead of night in an English cornfield.

Mind you, the live commentary, whispered in hushed, reverent tones over the background drone of the humming top, spiced things up a bit, interspersed with data from this machine and that bit of electronic gadgetry, which clearly showed a power of immense force at work here.

The fact that all their scientific kit was still packed away in its boxes at the back of the tent was neither here nor there. Their audience wanted to hear this stuff, and so hear it they would. They were loving every minute of it.

Georgie had long since taken his leave, having taken care to warn the crew not to approach the spacecraft — nor even to be spotted above the hedgerow. His insistence that two of his mates had already disappeared was more than enough to guarantee compliance, the crew having shoved the camera lens and microphone through the hedgerow, and hoped for the best before legging it.

Indeed, they were now commentating from the relative safety of their van, thanks to a very long piece of cable and a monitor screen, from the self-same images being screened thousands of miles away in Japan. Meanwhile the driver sat frozen to the steering wheel, his fingers on the ignition key, just waiting for the order to get the hell out of here.

Georgie had caught up with Ned a mile or so down the road, his hip pocket bulging with readies. He'd giggled every step of the way but, once back in the car, he just couldn't control himself any longer.

With the pair of them rocking from side to side, and tears streaming down their cheeks, it was quite impossible to start the engine, let alone drive home — not until they'd calmed down a bit. But each time Georgie managed to compose himself enough to get the engine started, just the slightest suggestion of a snigger from Ned would have him convulsing yet again.

A good belly laugh once in a while never did anybody any harm but, having made it their life's work, these two guffaw junkies were now seriously overdosed and in imminent danger of heart failure. The loud knock and the torch shining through the side window, however, very quickly brought them back to their senses.

"What the 'ell 'ee two buggers doin' out yer this time of night? An' 'ow the bloody 'ell did 'ee get past they road blocks?" wanted to know a rather harrassed PC Runstable, accompanied by a squad of very heavily armed soldiers.

Explanations would have to wait, this was no time for polite chit-chat, as the young Army Officer quickly reminded him. The giggles now well and truly locked away, Georgie started up the engine again and cleared off pretty damned smartish, with Runstable bringing up the rear to clear the area for the military.

Sappers had rigged up powerful arc lights all around the field, and were now awaiting Sir Gordon's command to switch them on. Behind the Sappers were armoured personnel carriers and tanks with flame throwers, their engines ticking over as their tense, highly trained crews listened for the command.

Ten miles away the Harriers circled in a holding pattern at an altitude of five thousand feet. In under two minutes from the Wing Commander's "Tally-ho", their smart bombs would be away and locked onto target, the co-ordinates of which were already programmed into their weapon systems computers.

The Prime Minister had steadfastly refused to allow Hot Lances to be mobilised. He shared Sir Gordon's anxiety about the mounting evidence, and feared extraterrestrial invasion as much as the next man, but he wasn't about to take the can back for unleashing nuclear devastation — not until all other avenues had been exhausted.

Those avenues were now poised and ready, as Sir Gordon studied the intruder through the light enhancing night sight. The green blur continued to echo its evil hum across the field, preparing the way for who knows how many millions more.

There was no doubt in Sir Gordon's mind that this was merely a reconnaissance craft, clearly from the same source as the monster investigated recently — and which was known to be still in the area. That it also contained some of those fearful 'lop' creatures was also not in dispute — but how many more of them were there, out there somewhere, just waiting for the all clear?

Well a good, sharp, kick up the arse would soon show them they weren't dealing with mugs — maybe then they'd clear off and find a softer victim to invade. Nuking the bastards to Kingdom Come would send the kind of message they'd understand but, with that hand tied firmly behind his back by lily-livered politicians, he'd have to make the most of what he had.

Giving the order to turn on the lights, so he could savour the spectacle from the safety of his tank, Sir Gordon called up the air strike. His command was acknowledged, also, by the tank and APC commanders, who now prepared to follow up and cremate anything which moved within the target zone.

Throughout Japan, from the cities to the villages, from the mountains to the sea shore, millions of tired eyes blinked in unison as the bright lights hit their screens. It took a second or two for the camera to react to the new lighting conditions but, by the time the crew had zoomed back to the wider angle shot, much clearer images of the spacecraft and its surroundings were bouncing off the satellite into the studio.

An entire nation held its breath, waiting for whatever was going to happen next. Were they about to witness, live, the emergence of beings from another planet? What message would they bring us from their leaders? Would they be able to communicate with us at all? A billion questions flashed through millions of minds, but of one thing they were all certain — our inter-gallactic visitors had come in peace. Why else would they have chosen the colour green?

They could have chosen any colour, including many outside the spectrum of the human eye — thus rendering themselves invisible to us — but they chose the colour we humans associate with peace. That, in itself, showed they understood us, and that their intentions were peaceable. And now they were about to show themselves.

The expectant viewers weren't kept waiting long for the next development. A series of increasingly loud whistles filled their ears, swiftly followed by brilliant flashes of light and deafening explosions. Through the dust and smoke appeared giant shafts of flame, belching forth from huge tanks as they trundled purposefully across the field.

There was no doubt that they were British. Neither was there any doubt about their purpose, or the success of their mission of total annihilation. As his nation mourned, the Japanese Prime Minister lodged his complaint, in the strongest possible terms, in the ear of the incumbent of No 10 Downing Street.

All that remained the following morning, amid the smoke and ashes of this famous victory, were the twisted chassis and mangled axle of Georgie's trailer, and tanks plastered with greengage jelly. Explaining those away as integral components of a spaceship was something even Sir Gordon wasn't about to try. He knew when he was beaten.

Throughout the corridors of power in Westminster and Tokyo, red faced diplomats scurried around, trying their best to soothe ruffled feathers. The Harrier crews at RAF Yeovilton were debriefed and stood down, and the giant tank transporters trundled their way back to Salisbury Plain.

The licence of the Japanese television company was revoked, with immediate effect, and their crew recalled. There would be no heroes' welcome.

All morning the Ministry of Defence had been trying, unsuccessfully, to contact Sir Gordon Bacon. His presence was required, urgently, in Whitehall, where the Prime Minister would like a word.

Sir Gordon had gone walkabout. He'd left his mobile phone, fax and telex equipment in the tank whilst taking an after-breakfast stroll to clear his mind.

"I may be some time" he told the tank commander, waiting to join the convoy. That he should quote Captain Oates, on his selfless suicide mission into the jaws of Antarctica, seemed a touch melodramatic to the tank commander. But he knew not to wait.

That his illustrious career was at an end was not in any doubt. The Ministry of Defence didn't suffer fools lightly, not if they'd been found out in the full glare of publicity. That kind of mud sticks and there were plenty to whom it might adhere with a passion, so the sooner the corpse was disposed of the better.

His only hope was that he might escape criminal

prosecution for the damage he'd done. But for that he'd need time to work out his defence, come up with a list of very senior people who'd give character references and plead mitigating circumstances on his behalf — there must be any number of them who owed him for covering up their past misdemeanours — and, if all else failed, prepare his escape route to South America.

Now filthy from the dust and smoke, his raincoat and trousers torn by the brambles he'd been scrambling through, and his shoes coated in thick, sticky mud, it was a very tired Sir Gordon who sat on the little bridge, contemplating his fate as he gazed into the river.

"Do 'ee wanna go fishin' or what?" asked Frankie, surrounded by his silent cousins who just stood, perfectly still, on one spot, staring at the dishevelled visitor.

"It'll be a tenner if 'ee do, an' extra for 'ire of tackle, an' extra for bait" quoted Frankie like a talking price list, his cupped left hand thrust forward in readiness.

Sir Gordon looked at the hand, and the left hands of all the others, and felt a very strong surge of déjà vu.

chapter 17

The diplomatic storm was still reverberating around the world several weeks later. The British Prime Minister hadn't taken too kindly to being woken in the middle of the night, nor to the accusations of being a senseless, murdering thug.

Britain had been made to look pretty foolish, an inexcusable situation for which heads had already rolled but, with the next round of GATT World Trade Talks due to begin in Tokyo shortly, Japan's over-dominant position would be considerably weakened should their own national gullibility remain the focus of media attention.

This situation suited most of the major trading nations of the world, and it was one which called for all the dexterity their politicians could muster. On the one hand they were whipping up anti-Japanese fervour at every conceivable opportunity, whilst on the other they were distancing themselves from the derision so created, presenting that inscrutable smile they'd learned from years on the receiving end.

The World's press had a ball. No longer were immigrant Poles the laughing stock of Americans, Belgians desisted from picking on the Walloons and even the English stopped taking the mick out of the Irish. All the old jokes came trotting out in pubs and bars everywhere, except this time they had a new slant as the Japanese took the brunt.

The media attention did the partners at Upper Clouts Farm Ltd no harm at all. Everybody wanted to see the remains of Georgie's trailer — on display at £1 a peep in what used to be the pigsty — while all the earlier attractions still took money hand over fist.

The car park had to be extended to accommodate the increased traffic, while the caravan park afforded overnighters the opportunity to gaze at the sky all night, waiting for the genuine extraterrestrials to return as they tucked into barbecued steaks from the newly opened Galaxy Grill.

The entire operation was now providing regular employment for over forty people, one of whom had been appointed to take charge of car parking — in return for his board and lodgings, plus a few pounds a week.

He was staying in the converted attic of Jack Marley's farmhouse, where he would amuse himself with a typewriter every evening until it was time for the household to turn in. He hardly ever spoke to anybody, but was never rude — he simply got on with his job of making sure the drivers had paid the parking fee, and that they didn't take up more space than was absolutely necessary.

He'd been taken on at Ned's insistence, even though both Jack and Georgie had been reluctant to take on a vagrant. They didn't even know his surname, and his habit of keeping his left hand in his pocket — even at meal times — seemed a little odd, but Ned had vouched for Gordon and that was good enough for his partners.

His typewriter was just about the only hold on sanity he had left. His wife had returned to Texas, but not before closing their bank accounts and having the house boarded up, along with everything in it — including his little Georgian silver box.

And having been stripped of both his job and his title, he was now reduced to scraping a living the best way he could. Old school chums in the publishing business had promised him the earth for his memoirs, but of course they couldn't part with a penny in advance royalties until they'd seen the finished manuscript.

He knew it was a forlorn hope, but it was the only hope left in his life and he needed something to cling onto. He could have done with access to his MOD files, to provide verification of some of the seemingly fantastic incidents he was about to reveal, but the MOD couldn't take away what was already in that photographic memory.

Joss' luminescent plastic spaceships were selling extremely well. Not only were the genuine space freaks buying them, but also those who'd just come for a laugh at the expense of the Japanese. For them Joss' little product was a replica of the greengage special, rapidly becoming a cult symbol of Japanese naivety but, when the accessories were introduced — a little plastic trailer complete with chassis and axle — sales quadrupled overnight.

Overtime was now a regular feature at Prossers and, with Christmas not too far away, Joss was the most popular man in the place since Sir Paul had passed away. This time, however, he wasn't about to let success go to his head. He'd already learned how fickle markets can be, and how quickly tomorrow's hero can become yesterday's fool, so he was taking just one day at a time.

Fleur was being far less sensible about the whole thing. She'd waited all her life for this miracle to happen and, now that it had dropped into her lap, she was going to make the most of it.

She surrounded herself with holiday brochures featuring exotic locations, picturing herself posing in a grass skirt on some Hawaiian beach, or maybe Joss limbo dancing in Trinidad. She gathered leaflets from estate agents on houses they couldn't afford to drive past, let alone buy, as she dreamed her dreams. Only this time they were for real.

Having realised the importance of the market place, Joss spent as much time at Upper Clouts Farm as he could manage. There he could pick up comments, see who were the type of people buying, and maybe come up with new ideas — like his trailer accessory pack.

But if these punters were to disappear again — due to no fault of his own — he'd be left high and dry with a factory full of totally useless junk. He needed to find other outlets for his products to safeguard against this, and was giving the matter some thought when part of Jack Marley's old barn collapsed.

We've all heard about the last straw which broke the camel's back, well in this case it was the lack of straw which was at the heart of the problem. For years the barn had withstood the worst the English weather could throw at it — even with several feet of snow on the roof it stood as solid as a rock.

But then it was full of straw, all neatly baled and stacked right to the roof. As demands on space for the new venture changed the face of the farmyard, the barn was pressed into service as a cafe and an extension of the shopping area, so the straw had to go.

Without the soft cushion to lean on, some of the tired old beams had begun to sag — until the time came for one of them to give up the ghost entirely. People screamed and dived for cover as half a ton of ancient oak heralded its intentions with an almighty crack, and just a few seconds later it smashed into the trestle tables below.

A small group of teenagers had been at the back of the

barn at the time, two of whom were now pinned by the legs under one of the tables. Jack dashed into the house to call the emergency services, but further cracking noises were heard from the roof as the extra load each remaining beam carried became the last straw.

The kids wouldn't stand a chance if that lot fell in on them, and there was little doubt that it would happen — long before the fire engine got there from Hampton.

With cracking and groaning noises filling the air, together with the screams of the trapped youngsters, Ned grabbed an iron bar and rushed into the barn. At the time he didn't have a clue what he was going to do with it, but it was the only implement lying around which looked remotely useful.

He was quickly followed by Joss, who had no idea why he'd gone in or what he could do to help, but it seemed like the right thing to do. Another crack, followed by the sound of corrugated iron roof sheets sliding off, gave a strong hint that time might not be on their side as Ned rammed the iron rod under the fallen beam.

Grasping the idea quickly, Joss dragged a log across the barn and placed it under the bar, before adding his own bulk to Ned's weight on the other end. They only managed to lever the oak beam a couple of inches off the ground, but it was enough to enable the teenagers to crawl free.

Supporting them as they limped out, Ned and Joss breathed a sigh of relief when they reached the fresh air, a sigh which was taken up in unison by the remaining beams as they finally succumbed to the superior force of gravity.

Jack was filling in his insurance claim by the time the emergency services arrived, and even got the firemen to post it for him on their way back, however the youngsters declined a trip to hospital in the ambulance, a badly sprained ankle being the worst of the injuries suffered.

Their little group were agricultural students from Holland, so fascinated by the corn circles that they'd come to see them for themselves. They believed they'd solved the mystery and would be exporting the phenomenon to the Netherlands, but not the ladders, ropes, planks and barrel hoops. They'd been stowed at the back of the barn and would now be totally useless, but they had no shortage of such implements back home.

The mystery they couldn't solve, however, was that of the white turnips and cabbages. There was just no way they were going to accept all that rubbish about spacemen — that was kids stuff — but as for an alternative solution, they were completely stumped. They all bought one of Joss' spaceships though, for their younger brothers and sisters of course.

Fleur felt very privileged when Argona had first invited her, and now the time had come she couldn't wait to experience it. She'd learned a great deal about life on Strontium already, but now she was about to receive live images — if Argona could get through.

Argona's mother was delighted to hear from her, she'd been thinking about her only the other day and was about to see if she could make contact herself. They'd only recently come out of their hibernation from the long winter, the days rapidly growing shorter as they headed for the long, hot, Castor Passover.

It was a change not to find her mother rushing around tidying up after her father, but then he didn't look as active as he once was. In fact he was looking decidedly old. She thought about asking her mother to stand in front of the mirror so she could see her, but thought better of it.

Mother was delighted to meet Fleur. She was a little alarmed initially by her sheer size, towering over her daughter by a very uncomfortable margin, but she could find no mallice in her at all. She thanked Fleur for her kindness in looking after the wanderers, and was pleased they'd found such sincere friends.

She was sitting in the garden, enjoying the shade of the big, old, Citrella tree with father, picking lomberries and amyaws for their tea. Father was a little grumpy. The rastors needed cutting back again — the blessed things seemed to take over during the long days which followed winter, and this year they were worse than ever.

He'd just have to tackle them the best way he could, but he wasn't looking forward to it one little bit. And it also seemed a bad year for wirtles for some reason, indeed much of the fruit she was preparing for tea was plagued with them. She really didn't like to use insecticides but there didn't seem to be much alternative.

Argona's brother had a new job. He'd been promoted. He worked at the Central Pool of Consciousness where his new job involved preparing the high sugar content food for the huge organism. It was a very responsible job because if it didn't get the right food, and in the right quantities, it would either wither and die or else bloat and become too lethargic to be of any use.

He wasn't allowed anywhere near the feeding centre itself, of course, although he'd been shown images of it. If he did his job well he could look forward to working there in another century or so. He was quite pleased with his new job though, altogether much cleaner than his old job at the other end of the site, where he'd worked for the last forty years or so.

And he was still able to enjoy his old perks as well, in fact he'd brought home several bags of the stuff only the other day. Father had yet to spread it over the garden, yet another job he was putting off — maybe that would help keep the wirtles under control.

As mother faded out — she just didn't have the energy for long chats, over such vast distances, these days — Argona knew that the time had come to prepare for the homeward journey.

"Fax coming through for you, Mr Stick, from a firm in Amsterdam we've not dealt with before. Does the name ring any bells with you?" asked Sarah.

Joss looked at the heading as the text spewed out of the machine, but SCHINKLER IMPEX bv meant absolutely nothing — not yet anyway.

Dear Mr Stick,

I understand I owe you a considerable debt of gratitude.

My daughter tells me your bravery helped save her life recently, and for that I am indeed truly grateful. I would very much like to thank you in person, if I may.

I also understand you are manufacturing a product which my daughter tells me is taking the United Kingdom by storm. I would very much like to see it, and maybe my company could market it worldwide.

If you are able to spare the time, perhaps you would care to visit Amsterdam to discuss the matter. If so, please ask your secretary to call me and I will make the necessary travel arrangements.

Thank you, again, for your prompt action in helping my daughter, and I look forward to meeting you.

Pieter Schinkler.

Joss thought about the invitation for all of a second and a half before asking Sarah to reply. It was true that he had a thousand and one things to do, and sparing the time for some foreign junket would be very hard to justify — but the opportunity of finding another outlet for his products was surely its own justification.

Late into the evening he worked away at his desk, preparing list after list of things that could possibly go wrong while he was away. The fact that he could be contacted, on his mobile phone, at virtually any point in his journey except while he was in the air, didn't seem to register — and neither did the fact that he would only be away from the office for one day. Joss was taking his responsibilities very seriously.

When he finally managed to drag himself away, he was devastated to hear the news that Yttrium and Argona were planning to return home. That they would some-day want to do that hadn't really occurred to either him or Fleur, but now the subject had been brought up he was unable to hide his disappointment.

They'd grown used to simply having them around and, although it hadn't really been all that long a time, it seemed as though they'd known each other all their lives. Without them life would be so empty, especially after all the help they'd given Joss.

Gradually his sorrow turned to panic, as Joss realised he couldn't just pick up the phone — mobile or other-wise — when he needed help and advice. There couldn't be any doubt that, without the help of his friends, he would not be in the position he was in today. Not only had they put him on the right track initially but, when the only market he had disappeared, who was it brought the punters flocking back to Upper Clouts Farm?

He certainly couldn't have sorted that problem out for himself, and he was equally sure there would be other — even tougher — problems ahead of him. Who would he turn to then?

That really isn't a problem, explained Yttrium. You have the same abilities as anyone else, all you lack is the practical experience — which you are gaining day by day — and belief in yourself.

That, perhaps, is the single most important element. Imagine what would happen if Argona and I doubted ourselves — especially whilst travelling in our vehicle. The entire system functions as an extension of our minds, so the consequences of self-doubt or indecision would be simply catastrophic.

Exactly the same applies to you. If you are not totally confident about what you are doing, the people around you will lack leadership and direction and, if that happens, equally disastrous consequences can be expected.

But if you are clear about what you want to achieve, and really believe in it deep down inside, you must communicate that certainty to everybody you come into contact with. They too will then believe in it and, just as important in the long term, they will believe in you.

When others believe in you it's much easier to sustain belief in yourself, even when things become a little tough, but the entire confidence trick starts and ends with you.

And don't forget to dream. The future of us all is destined and shaped by men and women of vision — but what makes them so special? They have the freedom to dream, as we all do from time to time, but they make dreams come true by believing in them — then seeing them through to reality.

If it wasn't for the dreamers, many of the things we take for granted today just wouldn't exist. Consider, for example, the very house we are sitting in. It didn't just materialise out of thin air, somebody wanted it to happen — they had a dream. The dream became plans, other people got involved and, slowly but surely, it became reality. Without that dream we'd be sitting in a field.

The more he thought about it, the more Joss realised the importance of dreaming. And if dreams really could become hard currency he was sitting on a fortune. Dreaming had been just about the only thing he'd been capable of until Yttrium came along — indeed he'd invested a lifetime in the practice, as Fleur and others had often pointed out. But now he could start turning some of them into reality.

Having total belief in himself, however, wasn't something that would happen overnight. Success would build upon success, that was something he could understand and accept, but there would be times when his self-confidence would falter. There would also be times when, no matter how hard he tried, he just wouldn't be able to dream up a solution. What should he do then?

He needed a life-line, some way of communicating with Yttrium when he was really up against it — but how on earth could he get in touch? After all, he didn't have the ability to communicate telepathically. That was about to change.

What you need to do, Joss, explained Yttrium, is begin by clearing your mind — totally. Absolute concentration is essential because just the slightest distraction will mean failure.

Then you must slowly start filling the void with the colour green. Let it permeate through every recess of your brain until your entire being is absorbed by it. Allow it to flood over you and flow through you until you are no more than a tiny green dot, awash in a vast river of deepest green.

Now you must direct the flow of the river. You will need to picture me, standing at the foot of a valley, and imagine the river heading straight for me. I will give you a small token to help you with this.

Borrowing Fleur's pinking shears, he cut a lock of his long, green hair, platting the strands to symbolise friendship. The ends he held between his thumb and forefinger, concentrating intensely until they glowed a bright red. There was no smoke, no fire, just a perfectly formed circle — symbolic of their eternal bond.

By holding this when making contact, it would enable the essence of Yttrium to flow through the river of green, helping it find its target. It would help Yttrium to have a personal token from Joss, something instantly associated with him.

Joss rolled him a joint.

chapter 18

Checking-in early for his 08.15 British Midland flight to Amsterdam, Joss was amazed to find so many people up and about at 6 o'clock in the morning.

Heathrow's Terminal One was even busier than Lime Street Station, but it seemed altogether brighter and more cheerful somehow. There were shops selling all manner of stuff — ties, socks, even plastic models of policemen — but quite who would want to buy a plastic policeman at 6 o'clock in the morning was beyond him.

Feeling just a little overcome by it all — not to mention more than a touch nervous at the prospect of his first, ever, flight — he just had to have a little sit down. He found a nice quiet corner in the smoking section of Harry Ramsden's Fish and Chip Emporium, and ordered a good old-fashioned Yorkshire breakfast with extra black pudding.

His flight was due to depart from gate 14, so he was advised to make certain he arrived there by about 8 o'clock. As that was only a quarter of an hour before the damned thing was due to leave, he decided to find out exactly where gate 14 was while he still had plenty of time. Leaving the Terminal building through the same door he'd used when he came in, Joss set off in search of the departure gates.

He couldn't find any gates at all — there were plenty of doors, dozens of them leading back into the building — but nothing looking remotely like a gate. Terminal One gradually merged into Terminal Two, but there were still no gates leading to the airfield.

"So 'ow the 'ell do you get to the soddin' gates, whack" he enquired, having eventually reached the head of the queue at the Quantas check-in desk. But when he finally reached Passport Control in Terminal Three, he got some very strange looks from the officials, who very quickly set him straight.

Eventually re-entering Terminal One, Joss looked at his watch. He was horrified when Mickey Mouse insisted it was ten past eight. Very hot and extremely flustered, he made straight for Passport Control as his name was being Tannoyed all over the building.

"Go immediately to gate 14 where your flight is waiting to depart" urged the faceless voice, repeating the message in case he was a little hard of thinking.

"'Ow the bloody 'ell can I with all these people in front of me, like?" screamed Joss at the loudspeaker, wondering why on earth it was necessary to put everybody's hand baggage through a car-wash — especially as the blasted thing wasn't working anyway.

They were just closing the door on the Boeing 737 as Joss came tumbling down the gangway, his tie askew and his shirt hanging out at the front, his sweaty face a vision of purple inelegance.

"Good morning, sir, would you be Mr Stick?" smiled the flight attendant as the door slid open, "May I see your boarding card please sir?"

The Senior Treasury Official travelling in the small, and very exclusive, Diamond Class section — neatly curtained off at the front of the aircraft — thought he'd struck it lucky on this flight. Not only did he have a spare seat alongside him — across which he'd sprawled the documents he intended to study on the journey — he also had a window seat he hadn't bargained for, having checked-in at the very last minute.

But as the ever-smiling flight attendant approached, accompanied by what appeared to be a sack of hammers with a beetroot poking out of the top, he knew it was going to be one of those days.

With his briefcase stowed by the flight attendant in an overhead locker, Joss smiled apologetically at his disgruntled neighbour and took his seat by the window. Almost immediately there was a strong surge of vibration, followed quickly by another, as the big jet engines screamed into life. Just a few minutes later, with Joss gripping the arms of his seat for dear life, the aircraft was on the move.

His apprehension wasn't helped when the flight attendant pointed out the emergency exits, then immediately started putting on a life jacket — showing him how to whistle to attract attention. He wanted to attract attention now alright, the kind of attention that would get him out of this sodding tin can, but he was so tense he couldn't even scream.

When he eventually opened his eyes and gazed out of the window, the green, green grass of England below him began to assuage his fear and he began to relax a little. For the first time, he began to feel the comfort of the deep, wide seat and, although the flight was a little bumpy, it wasn't nearly as bad as he'd expected. In fact it was really a rather nice sensation — he could quite get to like this.

The thunderous roar behind him had him gripping the seat in terror once again and, as the aircraft hurtled down the runway, he found himself pinned to the back of his seat. Terror turned to outright panic when the nose lifted and, through the tiny pane of glass separating him from eternity, he saw the ground begin to fall away below him.

The face which had, only moments before, been a deep shade of purple was now a ghastly white. It was still sweating, only now it was the icy cold sweat of sheer fright which ran freely from his troubled brow. If ever he needed Yttrium's help, it was now.

Reaching into his top pocket, he took out Yttrium's friendship token and tried to concentrate. Clear your mind of all distractions, he'd been told — but when you're up to your backside in Pit Bull Terriers it's sometimes just a little difficult to concentrate on sweeping out the kennels. This was clearly a skill which was going to need an awful lot more practice.

But just holding the token seemed to have a calming effect — certainly enough to enable him to let go of the Senior Treasury Official's arm — and when he began to think about the kind of journeys his friend had made, with black holes, comets and meteors to contend with, his own little ordeal seemed somehow more bearable.

When the ever-smiling flight attendant brought his breakfast — his second of the morning — the colour returned to his chubby little chops. He pulled the window blind down to help him concentrate on his meal — looking at the wrong side of clouds just wasn't doing much for his appetite at all — and by the time he'd finished his third cup of coffee the crew were preparing for landing.

Pieter Schinkler was delighted to meet him, and genuinely pleased he'd taken time out to travel to Holland. On the short drive into the city, pointing out the landmarks such flat terrain demands to ease its monotony, his host couldn't thank him enough for the bravery he'd shown. But he was equally keen to hear about Joss' luminescent plastic spaceships, especially now the Japanese connection had been established.

He showed his visitor around his new, computer controlled, warehouse, stopping occasionally to introduce him to his staff. It wasn't until he was introduced to a teenage lad, whose job it was to load the barges on the canal outside the warehouse, that Joss suddenly realised everybody he'd spoken to — the receptionist, the secretary, Pieter and all his warehouse staff — had spoken to him in English. And very good English at that.

"I am sweepink all de bollocks away vrom de doorway" smiled the lad as Joss and Pieter approached and, when Joss asked what he meant, he was shown a pile of rubbish. The expression had been gleaned from listening to English soccer fans, who used it whenever they disagreed with a refereeing decision but, when Pieter quietly explained the facts of life to him in Dutch, the lad went very red indeed.

Pieter's office was simply palatial. White leather armchairs encircled a low, glass-topped coffee table, while at the other end of the room the vast mahogany desk, with white leather chairs on either side, fronted the huge windows looking out across the canal onto the Beatrixpark.

Joss wondered if he should take off his shoes before stepping onto the plush, white, carpet, but his momentary delay was quickly curtailed as his host ushered him across to the coffee table. On the table sat a very plain, wooden, cigarette box — which Pieter proffered as his secretary brought in the coffee.

"Do you smoke, Joss?" enquired Pieter politely.

"Oh, ta very much whack" smiled Joss, equally politely. "I ran out this mornin', like, an' I never got time to pick up me duty frees."

"No", laughed the Dutchman, "I mean do you smoke?" he repeated, pointing at the box.

When Joss opened the box of ready made joints he couldn't believe his eyes — or his nose. He simply stared at the things in utter disbelief, before peering over his shoulder to see if the secretary was watching.

"Relax, Joss, you are in Holland now" beamed his increasingly genial host. "We have a different attitude to these things in my country. When my government legalised cannabis the profit motive disappeared — and so did the playground pushers. Now we are all happy, very happy." He took one himself and offered Joss a light.

The pair were totally relaxed and completely on the same wavelength, chatting away like long-lost friends when Joss remembered the reason for his visit. Reaching into his briefcase he pulled out one of his plastic spaceships, tossed it to Pieter, and invited him to throw it onto the glass table.

As he did so, the little spaceship began to fluoresce with a magical green glow, a glow which reflected in Pieter's smiling, appreciative face. He knew exactly where he could place these, and lots of them, if Joss was prepared to negotiate mutually exclusive world-wide marketing rights. You bet your boots he was.

Over lunch they discussed the finer points of the contract, a process Joss found surprisingly easy. Both men needed to profit from the relationship and, with a little give and take on both sides, it wasn't difficult to reach an agreement which ensured this would happen. With honour mutually satisfied, each man having given more or less as much as he had got, Pieter offered his new business partner a quick tour of the sights before taking him back to the airport.

He knew precisely which area Joss would find the

most interesting and, having parked the car in the multi-storey car park on Beurs Plein, the pair set off on foot around the little red light district.

Prostitution is not exactly unheard of in Liverpool, so it was no surprise to find that Amsterdam had such an area. What was surprising, though, was that the girls displayed their wares in shop windows for all to oggle at. After the initial shock, Joss found it all a huge joke and, when he spotted a butcher's shop, with its little window filled with dead meat and flanked on either side by a brothel, he couldn't resist a little snigger.

He found the little cafes in the district highly fascinating, not so much for the food and drink available, but for the wide variety of cannabis products on sale. No little twists of paper surreptitiously changing hands in dark alleyways, with buyer and seller constantly looking over their shoulders, here the entire process was completely out in the open.

He was even shown a museum dedicated to the production of cannabis, the little building overlooking the Achterburgwal sporting a live marijuana plant, growing under lights in its front window. The seeds, the plants, and even the lights were for sale, together with horticultural instructions in any language you might care to mention. Heaven, he concluded, must be around here someplace.

His flight home was an altogether more relaxed affair. The fact that he was as high as a kite — even while the aircraft was still on the ground — undoubtedly helped but, more important, he'd managed to overcome his fear of flying without having to trouble Yttrium. Neither had he needed any help in negotiating the deal, one which would secure the future of Prossers for quite some time. At long last, Joss was beginning to believe in himself.

The river level at Farthing Fflitch dropped by a good couple of feet within the space of less than ten minutes. Frankie wouldn't have noticed had it not been pointed out by one of his customers, but the keep net full of wriggling trout was now several inches above the waterline.

The reason could be found a mile or so upstream, where the vehicle was being made ready for the return journey, concentrating vast quantities of water to add to the nutrients from Upper Clouts Farm. It would be a long trip but much of it would be spent in hibernation, relaxing in the deep, warm, interior lining.

Joss and Fleur had never seen anything like it, and neither would they again. They'd been quite astounded as the river boulder grew and grew, the sheer size of the thing defying any expectations they may have had. But once inside it, they were amazed not to find the banks of instruments and computers they just assumed would be there.

There weren't even any windows, just that lining of warm, comfortable, plasma jelly — and the umbilical cords connecting the entire system to the navels of its pilots. It was a little cramped inside, especially for Fleur, but once she was able to relax and lie back, allowing the jelly to mould itself to her shape, she soon succumbed to its sensual delight.

Preparing for take-off, Joss and Fleur began to receive Argona's mental images — it was just as if they were flying the thing themselves. More to the point, it was as if they were all flying together without the aid of the vehicle, those purple Strontian eyes seeing right through the plasma.

Over the treetops they sailed, effortlessly and silently, the animals in the fields below running for cover as the huge vehicle soared overhead.

The anglers on the riverbank watched, open-mouthed, as it glided gracefully over Farthing Fflitch, casting its gigantic shadow as it passed. Yet another fishing tale was born, one that would live on in the riverside pubs for years.

Frankie cursed himself for not having replaced his broken shotgun. His best chance ever of bringing down one of those sodding balloons, and he was too tight fisted to buy himself a new gun. He could easily afford it, money was rolling in like it had never rolled in before. And it would continue to roll in, thanks to the tiny sliver of plasma left in the river — a parting gift from distant cousins.

Gordon was the first to spot it from Upper Clouts Farm. He'd been patiently putting up with a lecture from a German circle enthusiast, convinced the patterns were no more than a poor, man made, copy of Sumerian hieroglyphics, first used by tribesmen on the Iraqi border five thousand years ago.

The Teutonic tirade continued unabated, cursing the stupidity of the English who believed in flying saucers, when logic clearly dictated that life couldn't possibly exist elsewhere in the universe — and that even if it did, there was simply no way such vast distances could be travelled.

The stunned silence when Gordon simply pointed to the horizon was beautiful to behold, a silence quickly taken up by everyone else at the farm. The hustle and bustle of punters and puntees ground to a halt, the entire assembly gazing with awe-struck reverence as the vehicle floated in towards them.

Many fell to their knees as it came to rest overhead, simply hovering over the complex of souvenir stalls and rides, corn circles and whitened crops. All traffic on the lane outside ground to a halt, but not a single horn was sounded as the rubber-necked drivers craned their heads skyward in sheer wonderment.

Georgie nudged Ned, who stuck his elbow in Jack's ribs as he looked up from his calculator.

"Money from 'eaven" whispered Jack, misquoting the Bible. His partners knew exactly what he meant — a meal ticket for life. Georgie was already wondering how many one square foot plots they could get out of the ten acres, and how much your average punter would pay for his or her own piece of the Spaceport.

None of them would ever have to work again, that was absolutely certain, but Ned would probably be the only one to enjoy retirement. He'd spend all day, every day, propping up the bar at the Shafton Arms — knowing full well that Georgie would still be at the other side of the bar. It was in his blood.

And Jack would spend the rest of his days with a calculator in one hand and a phone in the other, giving earache to some poor stockbroker until he either made another fortune — or lost the one he had.

Gordon, on the other hand, didn't know whether to laugh or hide. He'd been right all along about the existence of this thing — but had he also been right about its intentions? Right now he was powerless to do anything about it, without so much as a slingshot to defend the people against this Goliath. But somehow he didn't feel at all threatened, in fact a very deep peace was beginning to engulf him as he gaped at the wondrous sight overhead.

Allowing his mind to wander freely, he caught the most amazing glimpses of the scene below the vehicle — as if he was actually in it. He could see himself waving now, trying to attract the attention of the occupants, three of whom he could see quite clearly.

Two of them were human, of that he was convinced, but the other seemed to be some kind of dwarf, with almond-shaped purple eyes. There was a familiarity to those eyes he just couldn't place. He knew he couldn't possibly have seen them before and yet, somewhere, in the depths of his existence, there was a hint of recognition.

Slowly the vehicle descended as the crowd moved back out of its way, still transfixed by the scene they were privileged to witness. The interior was awash with tears, as heart-felt hugs and tender kisses were followed by final, and very painful farewells. This was no 'au revoir', it was goodbye.

It was an extremely red-eyed Joss who slid out first, ready to catch his distraught wife and stop her stumbling on the concrete hardstanding. As she collapsed into his arms, averting her tear-soaked eyes from the inevitable departure, the vehicle slowly ascended.

All eyes except hers remained locked onto the green dot as it gained altitude, but it was gone long before its image faded from a single retina.

From somewhere out in space, Joss and Fleur shared their friends' final glimpse of Earth, the brilliant blue colour of the rapidly disappearing planet shining out like a jewel against the black emptiness through which it travelled.

The image was crystal clear, unlike that of Argona's reflection as she wiped away the tears.

Gordon experienced the same images, although he wasn't quite sure where the reflection was coming from. It looked like a small piece of aluminium foil, but it couldn't possibly be — could it? And the hand that was holding it — he could have sworn it had six digits.

"Sierra Foxtrot from Foxtrot Thirteen" squawked the radio on Sergeant Roberts' desk.

"Go ahead, Runstable" replied the long-suffering Sergeant.

"'Ere Sarge, 'ee ain't gunna believe this, but . . ."

Also published by CALLEVA:

SHAFTON ROSE

by

Ray Bullock

ISBN 0 952 1051 0 1

Seldom have I read a book and laughed so much. Excruciatingly funny, unbelievable yet believable. I couldn't put the book down.
ADAM KIRTLEY, BBC RADIO BERKSHIRE

As sharp and fruity as a home-brewed cider, and a rollicking cheery read it is too! I look forward to meeting these characters again.
RICHARD KIRKMAN, READING EVENING POST

Rumbustious...zany...full-blooded! Ray Bullock will be most appreciated by the many fans of Tom Sharpe and his hilarious WILT and BLOTT ON THE LANDSCAPE best sellers.
NIGEL PARKES, SOUTHERN EVENING ECHO